Steve Schwartz was born and raised in New York City. He is a journalist and amateur musician and lives in the Netherlands.

He should not be confused with composer and lyricist Stephen Lawrence Schwartz, however much he might want to be.

To Molly, my fellow listener.

It strikes me that this may be one of the differences between youth and age: when we are young, we invent different futures for ourselves; when we are old, we reinvent different pasts for others.
—Julian Barnes, *The Sense of an Ending*

"Art is the only thing that matters…. In comparison with art, wealth and rank and power are not worth a straw."
—W. Somerset Maugham, *The Alien Corn*

He was already dead… The consequences of every act are included in the act itself.
—George Orwell, *1984*

Knew It All Along

A History of Music

S.D. Schwartz

I DON'T BELIEVE THAT, as I made my first delivery to the Hermit, I could be blamed for failing to see that nothing would be the same again. To say he changed my life might border on the dramatic. To say anything else would diminish his memory.

As a teenager I could not fathom his depth. I could not imagine his knowledge of and sadness at the world, that he could continue to exist without either exploding in pain or being crushed entirely by it. The heights and the disappointments. Inside his frail frame I saw a giant hiding, though I could never understand how his brittle body could possibly sustain it. Even now, as I feel age gnawing at my own carriage, the intensity he bore seems to me too much to impose upon any person.

The Hermit was a living history of the twentieth century. He was heaved high on the shoulders of its achievements and ravaged by its tumult. Without raising his voice he caught the ear of anyone who had any comprehension of beauty and then rejected their attention as false and uncomprehending. He doubted everything, believed no one, accepted nothing at face value. It was what made him an artist, and then what destroyed the artist. Without ever knowing it, the Hermit was one of the creators of the modern era, and one of its casualties.

"So, my young friend, you have returned."

"So I have." In fact, I return to you nearly every day. I would continue to show up at your door if you were still there to return to.

"Why? What do you hope to find here?"

"Then? Or now? Then? My future. Now, of course, my past. Or, better said, the past I never had."

The Hermit examines me as he had all those years ago. When he does, I am thirteen again. As I return, I am thirteen now.

⸉

WE LIKE TO REMEMBER the nineteen-sixties as a time of love and peace. We cling to the idealism expressed in floppy hats, muslin bell-bottoms, daisies painted on faces. In fact it was first a decade of hate and war. Of course, now is also a time of hate and war—every time is. We choose to remember the sixties differently because people responded to the hate and war differently. But make no mistake, there was plenty of hate and war.

For me, though, it was a time of music.

I was born to the clash and rhyme of music. To the cacophony and chorus of the streets of New York City. To chaos and harmony. To the consonance and disarray of chords and melody. To tiny passages that still tear my soul apart. To rock songs and classical symphonies that make me go hot all over or freeze right through. I was shaken awake by all the anticipation and enthusiasm and innocence and hope embodied in the first chord of "A Hard Day's Night." But I was also awakened by images of Black Americans being half-drowned by the vengeful jet of fire hoses on the streets of Birmingham, Alabama, and of Vietnamese villages torched by American soldiers, the life dashed out of their eyes.

Everything I witness is accompanied by an internal soundtrack. Even now, I can think about the unthinkable violence committed against civil rights protesters in the American South and hear behind it a gospel choir singing...

Free at last, free at last
Thank God Almighty I'm free at last

…joyous even amidst the destruction and pain.

I won't say that without "A Hard Day's Night" I'd never have woken up. But it was the *best* way to wake up—the best way I can imagine, anyway. It was this confusing-delightful *crash* that blew my eyes open. It awakened me to the love of music. The sex of music. The drug of music. All of a sudden, I understood that there was more, and I had to know more. I wanted to know what came before that wonderful chord to have made it possible. And I wanted to know what came after. I wanted to know how music, this thing that we cannot touch or taste, could make me feel like *this*. Alive.

I am a native of the Woodstock nation. I learned young to question authority. I learned to rebel against my parents even more than the Elvis Generation had done in its time. I learned to hate government. So, the love I was taught by the culture of love was also the product of hate.

I was an angry youth but I wasn't an angry person. I marched and shouted against the war in Vietnam, but I learned to say please and thank you in the grocery store and to give up my seat on the bus to old people. I played Beatles songs on the guitar but I also practiced Bach Two-Part Inventions on the piano. In reality, my greatest act of rebellion consisted of playing records a little too loudly in my bedroom.

My piano teacher heard that I had an ear and encouraged me to develop my talent by picking out songs on the piano. I chose "Comin' Thro' the Rye." My brother, of the Elvis Generation, was quick to point out that "Comin' Thro' the Rye" was Holden Caulfield's song. I didn't particularly like Holden Caulfield. He could never love the precision of the young George Harrison, or the passion of Little Richard, or even the strength and clarity of Isaac Stern. He liked "Comin' Thro' the Rye" for its lyrics, not for its music. I think he would have liked The Kinks' "Well-Respected Man" too, because it was about everything that's phony, and that's what he hated. I liked "Well-Respected Man" because the rhythm throws you off balance. The rhythm says *we're not conforming*. I found that much more important than the lyrics.

I chose "Comin' Thro' the Rye" because it is sweet and melodic. I should say, I know *now* that it is sweet and melodic. I can say I love that song because it has a deceptive complexity. I can tell you about its unusual theoretical makeup in ways I could never have described as a teenager. I was only just opening my eyes. I just liked the song.

Of course, love and peace were pleasant enough ideals. At age thirteen, though, they were not nearly as important to me as getting hold of more money than my mother would, or could, give me for my weekly allowance. I needed more records. One week it was Motown, the next it was Baroque music from the dollar-ninety-nine cent rack at Sam Goody's in Midtown Manhattan.

I liked to think of myself as a normal kid. I liked playing punchball in the playground with my friends. I had a healthy hatred of my school teachers. I watched stupid television. But I realize now that I had a secret side. Who knows? Maybe all kids have a secret side. If my friends had that, they were keeping it *very* secret, because I only saw them playing in the playground, hating our teachers, and watching stupid television.

Me? I had something else—a hunger I could not explain.

I would close the door to my bedroom and tune my guitar for hours at a time, tightening and loosening the strings until not a beat was left between them. If I couldn't get every vibration out of each interval, I would detune all of it and start again.

I taught myself how to play "House of the Rising Sun" by playing the Animals' record over and over. It took me days to learn to play the B seven chord without any of the strings buzzing, and many more to learn to make the transition from G Major to B seven to E Minor, and weeks before I could do it without hesitating, and months before I could do it without looking. I would play the chords until the most strident pain developed in my fingertips. That I found infuriating. My mother told me it was "just" a broken blood vessel in my fingertip and it happened to all starting string players. She said to let it rest and start again. I took her reassurances as belittlement. I would not be comforted. The only thing better than listening to music was making music. It didn't matter if it—if I—was reduced to two chords. But if my fingers hurt too much, then I was reduced to listening. *Reduced*, I realize, is an inappropriate word because I *had* to listen to music. I had no choice. But I had music to listen to. The radio would do in a pinch, but the pop stations became tiresome as they had the habit of playing the same songs in a kind of mindless repetition. I couldn't switch to WQXR to listen to classical music without going into the living room—my transistor radio played only AM—and my music was a private experience. I didn't want my mother or brother listening in.

I needed more records. I would have to find a job.

I knew the people at the delicatessen around the corner. I went there every Sunday morning to pick up smoked whitefish, lox, pastrami, rye bread, pumpernickel, coleslaw, and mustard—all wrapped hermetically in heavy white paper—for my mother's weekly gathering of artists and literati. Everyone would chip in a dollar—or a six-pack of cream soda or Cel-Ray Tonic—and then, over a bulging sandwich, bemoan culture as they knew it sinking into the quagmire. The group chose to descend on our house after my mother plunked a giant, second-hand dining table in the middle of our living room. Her logic was simple, if not universal. A Jewish family lives in the kitchen—the kitchen *is* the living room. By extension, the living room is where we eat. And so it was. Conversely, the "dining alcove," as the landlord had dubbed it while showing us around, contained a two-seater couch and a small TV poised on a stack of balsa fruit crates. The living room—sorry, dining room—was also our music room. It held a baby grand piano and chairs for the quartets my mother played every Wednesday evening. When we put in the leaves for Sunday brunch, the music stands went under the piano and the music chairs became dining chairs.

At our brunches I mostly just listened to the conversation filled with Sartre and Ferlinghetti and…

"History repeats itself, first as tragedy, then as farce."

"From the first day to this, sheer greed was the driving spirit of civilization."

"Have you read 'Christ Climbed Down'?"

"I'm still trying to digest 'I saw the best minds of my generation…'"

…though I knew instinctively that they could not be talking about *ma-ma-ma-My Generation*.

All of it was accompanied by the ever-present classical music on the hi-fi. The food was delicious. The white paper packages became serving trays on the table and the room filled with the smells of caraway seed rye bread and coffee. My mother's friends were good to me and were careful to include me in the conversation. What with my father absent and my mother teaching full-time, all the people around the table had agreed—whether tacitly or expressly, I never knew—on some kind of tag-team system with which to offer me more parental attention. Jack, a staff writer for the *Empire Review*, took me to baseball games. Sometimes he took me along when he had a film to write up. Harold was an architect, I think. Sometimes I went across the street to his apartment to look at his latest drawings and mockups. Rubie, who lived upstairs, taught school. She taught me origami and macramé. She had paintings on easels scattered strategically around her apartment, though they never seemed to change or progress. She told me that some famous jazz musician had written a song for her.

My mother said she was bending the truth about that, but it made a good story. All I knew was that she was beautiful.

All the activity didn't completely fill in for the father I only knew from two grainy black-and-white photos, but I suppose it helped. We also had a record of him performing the Beethoven Violin Concerto in front of an unknown orchestra. He had, to the best of anyone's knowledge, made exactly one record and it had not sold well, if at all. My mother called it a collector's item. Her sardonic tone went right past me. I listened to the record a few times, but the sound quality was poor and I didn't come away feeling like I knew him any better for it. All I knew was that he had been a violinist and, apparently, not good enough. I did not feel myself missing my father. I didn't experience a longing for him to return home. He had never been home, not in my lifetime. He was, as far as I was concerned, composed of a photograph and an LP—and neither of them of exceptional quality.

I liked that time. I found adults strange and fascinating creatures. They spoke an odd language. Their way of thinking was unlike anything I came across in my world. Just the idea that eating and talking was their main form of play was, to me, nothing less than bizarre. But I felt inexplicably attracted to them, and equally relieved that I could retreat to the world of my friends and my music.

Still, anxious to boost my weekly income, I finally plucked up the courage to ask the people at the delicatessen for a job. Mrs. Kahanah, who stood behind the counter, thought I was a *very* nice boy and she told me so—every week. "*So* polite. *Such* good mannahs. It's a shame ya not a couple years oldah," she said—every week. "Yud make *such* a match for my dawdah." The daughter in question was three years older than I and weighed about a hundred pounds more, so I was able to just nod and smile and think, *not in this lifetime*. My disinterest in the chopped liver heiress notwithstanding—or perhaps in the hope that I would change my mind—they were thrilled to offer me a position as a delivery boy.

I took possession of an enormous bicycle equipped with a woven metal basket on the front with which to take orders to people in the neighborhood. ("Tell me if it's too fah. I'll run it over in da cah.") School was out, the weather had turned warm, and I loved tooling around Greenwich Village on the thing. The streets, the trees, the traffic all seemed to echo the theme of "An American in Paris" of their own accord. Even now, Abingdon Square sings "My mom gave me a nickel to buy a pickle" to the melody of *La Matchiche*.

I got fifteen cents for each delivery, plus tips, often another dime. It meant that I couldn't join in as many pickup punchball games at the Gansevoort Street playground. But, I kept a pink rubber ball—called a Spaldeen—in the pocket of my dungarees in case the opportunity arose. Even in a time of music, a young teenage boy needs something to smack. Given the remotest chance, I'd join an ongoing game if only for an inning. Someone was always glad to have me pinch-hit. I loved to loft the ball, draw back my fist, and drop it in behind second base for an easy single. A new Spaldeen rang out an almost perfect B-flat as it left my knuckles.

Friday afternoon at the deli was always busy and earned me the cash I desired. If there was a lull in the action, I sat at a table across from the drinks case, read Superman comics, and listened to the transistor radio tuned to play Peggy Lee, Rosemary Clooney, Bobby Darin, and Nat King Cole. It was lively music, complex at times. Mostly though, I found it old-fashioned and uninteresting. In any case, I've never heard so many different versions of "Cry Me A River" before or since. The music was hanging on for dear life to an earlier style of song by and for an older generation. The fifties had started in post-war euphoria and ended in Cold War fear. All these crooners could do was shout, each louder than the last, "I'm not afraid of Communism and I'm certainly not afraid of Joe McCarthy." The happier they sounded, the duller the music got. The more they told me that everything was coming up roses, the more I doubted them.

{

MY MOTHER'S BROTHER, my Uncle Dave, had a cottage near a lake in the Catskill Mountains about two hours north of the City. We could use it when he took his family to Europe, sometimes for a couple of weeks, sometimes for a month, sometimes the whole summer. The Lake had cottages along two sides, a pine forest at the far end, and a tiny beach at the near approach. It was a place to swim and cool off from the cruel heat of the city. One local guy had half a dozen ten-foot sailing dinghies tied up to a dock, which we could rent for a dollar for the afternoon. I wasn't particularly good, but it was fun going out with Simon, skimming over the lake when the breeze was up, listening to the rhythms that the water played against the thin metal hull. Most evenings we were able to pull enough kids together to play softball in a field that worked as a cow pasture during the day. Pretty often we teamed up city kids against the townies. In my memory, those summers were the only times Simon and I really played together.

There was an upright piano in the living room of my uncle's cottage, but it was too out of tune to use.

"Why don't they have it tuned?"

My mother shrugged.

"Well, we could have it tuned."

She shrugged again.

But the inability to play piano allowed me to fill my head with other music, probably more than if I'd had a working piano in range. I took my guitar along, so at least I could practice my Beatles and Stones and Dylan. Playing guitar was one more thing to do with the kids there. There was a fire pit near the lake which was perfect for some loud singing. The adults sang "Michael, Row Your Boat Ashore." We sang "Twist and Shout."

Nights were devoted to reading comics, listening to the Top Forty on the local AM station, catching fireflies. But I also liked walking around the lake at night. Listening to the sounds. The City had sparrows and pigeons and little else. In the mountains, I learned to identify chickadees, screech owls, and a few frogs. And something that sang a high E-flat—nothing else—every six seconds.

The night allowed me to smell the pine trees when the wind nuzzled them. Or to lie on my back under the sky, hold up a blue paper map with furry beasts printed on it, and try to figure out the constellations until my arms got tired.

Uncle Dave lived out on Long Island during the year so we didn't see him much. Sometimes, if he had to keep working, his kids would join us at the lake and we'd double up in the bedrooms. They were nice, very different from Simon and me. They were what I thought of as pretty typical suburban kids—sheltered and innocent to the ways of the big city—but we managed to have fun. I've fallen out of touch with Sarah. Jon and I email each other to say Happy Birthday, Happy Hanukkah.

My mother said she couldn't do without the summer school money. The son-of-a-bitch-landlord-prick had put up the rent again and still never got around to fixing the leaking bathroom sink. The tap had carved a green teardrop into the enamel layer of its sunken face—always wet, ever in mourning for a home that did its best to remember its own faded prestige, its tarnished reputation. The Blanche DuBois of brownstones, best seen in the dark. My mother grumbled about speculators. She said this old dump would be worth a million one day. This place?

Finally, Simon and I were allowed to go to the Lake without my mother. It had the advantage of being away from her, and the drawback that we were guests. Even if they were family, it was their house and it wasn't ours. We would go for three weeks, not longer—my mother's rule.

But it was fun taking the train up to Poughkeepsie. We had arranged a meeting spot in the station parking lot and squeezed into my uncle's car, three of us in the back seat and Simon in front next to my Uncle Dave.

Sometimes I wondered if my mother had ever asked her brother for money and he had refused. Or if he had ever offered her money and she had refused. Money and wealth were less visible to me as a teenager, but they were not invisible. In the City, there were kids who went to summer camp. At the Lake, there were kids who had their own summer cottages. And there were kids who never left the Catskills all year long—kids who had never been down to New York City. We didn't have a second home but neither did we live in the slums of East New York. I was aware of that. I didn't hold it against rich kids that they were rich. I hoped they didn't treat me differently.

ALL OF THIS IS TO tell of the first delivery I made for the delicatessen. It was the owner, Mr. Kahanah, who referred to him as the Hermit. "A nice enough guy, mind you. I'm not one to judge. But, alone in that house all the time—so dark, so lonely."

The Hermit lived in a brownstone on Charles Street, below the stairs where the addresses are appended by "and-a-half." I knew a few people who lived at the "and-a-half" addresses. These were indeed dark apartments though many drew light from a small garden in the back.

The door did not have an electric bell, only a heavy cast-iron knocker. I had to balance the pot roast on one arm while swinging the dead weight up and down. I tapped it four times, slowly, and heard the first four notes—four taps on the tympani, *mezzo-piano*—of the Beethoven Violin Concerto.

I waited for a long time, probably half a minute, aware of the fact that the pot roast was wrapped in white cardboard tubs and would soon start seeping through. I reached to knock again but a deadbolt snapped from the inside. The door opened slowly and a tiny, elderly man peered out. A gray wrinkled man, stooped and slow in his movements. I guessed him to be in his seventies but, as I was thirteen, he could have been fifty—or a hundred—and I wouldn't have known. He wore a button-down shirt, trousers that looked like they came from a suit, and brown leather slippers. He had to tilt his head sideways to look at me. For just a moment I found myself speechless. His face was without expression. I wondered whether you need facial expressions if you live alone and never go outside. He turned his eyes to my package and his face broke into a gentle smile.

"Come in. *Come in*. That must be heavy." It wasn't but I felt relieved all the same. Relieved that he wasn't a creep. Or dead. Or something.

We walked through a tiny vestibule just large enough to hold a coat rack into his living room. He turned and tilted his head up to say, "Wait here, please." He had a slight accent, whether British or Russian I had no clue. But, all at once he had a past. He was a person.

He lifted the food from my arm and took it into his kitchen just off the living room. He went to another room beyond, I guessed in search of money.

At that age, I was unable to stand still for very long. I walked over and looked at his record collection which took up several long shelves. They were alphabetized by composer. Arensky, Bach, Beethoven, Brahms, Elgar, Franck, Grieg and on down to Wieniawski, and a bunch of others I had never heard of. (Was "Y-Say-Ye" really a name?) Hundreds of records. That was what I wanted. Maybe not all *these* records, though I was suddenly curious to know what they held. Next to them was a bookshelf with titles by Bruno Walter and Leonard Bernstein, two names I did recognize, and many more that I did not. I could hear the old man wandering around and muttering to himself. Or was he singing? I began to wonder if he had forgotten about me.

There was a grand piano across the room from where I was waiting. It was not shiny black like the one we had at home. It was dark brown and had a deep grain that made it look more like a piece of furniture. It was longer than the one we had at home. I opened the fallboard and pressed lightly on a key. The three strings that combined to make one note waged a painful battle. I winced at the sour sound and removed my finger as soon as it registered.

The man ambled into the room, smiled, and said, "Beautiful, isn't it?" My mother had taught me very young not to touch things in other people's houses. I felt embarrassed and put the lid back down as quickly as I could without letting it slam. He dropped his head to one side in an attempt to catch my gaze. He was still waiting for an answer.

"Um, yeah."

He lost his smile—even though I wasn't looking at him, I could hear it in his voice. "Are you being polite or do you just have a bad ear?"

I met his gaze and forced a smile. "I guess I'm being polite."

He smiled and nodded. "It's probably ten years or more since I had it tuned."

I think I must have looked like I had just bitten into a lemon. "Why not?"

He cocked his head to the other side and shrugged with his eyebrows. "Why yes? I don't play it, nor does anyone else."

"You never played it?"

"Not really. I was a violinist." The tiniest smile came to his face and he looked out the window. "All of my pianists are dead."

I looked back and forth between him and the piano. "Well, but, why do you keep it?"

He paused for a second. "Ah, a good and honest question. In all fairness, I must confess that I'm not sure. Nostalgia, I suppose." He examined my face. "Do you know what I mean?"

"I guess not."

He smiled. "What can someone your age feel nostalgic about? Maybe I can explain it to you sometime."

I turned to examine the piano again. It was about six feet long and beautiful to look at. There was not a speck of dust on it and it still bore a deep polish.

He took a step closer. "If I have it tuned, will you play it?"

I felt my eyes widen. "How do you know I play piano?"

Again that eyebrow shrug. "Just a guess. You know where Middle C is." He chuckled. "Or where it's supposed to be." He turned to straighten a small print hanging on the wall. "Are you Jewish?"

"Well, I work for the kosher deli."

He smiled. "That's not what I asked."

I blushed. He looked at me again.

"Now, in all fairness to *my* honest question…"

I blushed again. Why was I doing all this blushing? "Yeah, we're Jewish, but not very."

"Not very." He nodded. "Not very. So, tell me, Mister

Not Very—"

"Michael."

"Ah, so tell me, Michael, do you like music?"

"I like it a lot." I tried to keep the enthusiasm out of my voice but failed. Still, I couldn't bring myself to say I loved music passionately. As a teenager I was not prepared to openly love anything.

"So!" He smiled fully. "Now that we have established that you're Jewish—*if only not very*—you live in a, shall we call it, a comfortable part of town?"

"We're not rich or anything."

"No, no. Of course not. But you get along all right. You don't go hungry."

Was he making fun of me?

He thought a moment and sat on his couch. "You seem to come from an educated family."

I was mildly uncomfortable witnessing my own dissection. At the same time, I felt the same enjoyment I derived from watching Basil Rathbone deduce that his guest had just arrived on the nine-seventeen from Reading.

"So!" he repeated, "if we know that you come from an educated, comfortable." He held up his hand to say *stop*. "I know, *not rich*, Jewish family," he sighed, "would it be fair to guess that you take piano lessons?"

I thought about this for a moment. "I have friends like that, friends like me, who don't take piano lessons."

He lay his head on the back of the couch and considered that. I could tell it seemed like a new idea to him.

"Ah, and how sad for them. No music in their lives?"

"Well, they all love music." It was all right to say that *they* loved music. "I guess most of them had piano lessons for a year or two but then they gave up."

"But you did not. Why not?"

If I had not been a teenager, I could have told him about all the things that music did to me. How I heard music in my head all the time. How it pulled every emotion out of me, including many I could not name. How I needed to have music around me all the time. I felt my lip quiver and hoped he hadn't seen it.

"I really have to get back to the deli."

"Of course, how silly of me." He rose and gave me fifteen cents. I took it but I didn't want to. I wanted to thank him though I didn't know why.

DAYS PASSED AND the Hermit's face and voice followed me through my house, through the streets, through my sleep. He had spoken words that should have, or could have, hurt my feelings but did not. Why did he say those things? I ran through all the possibilities in my head. He lived alone and had lost touch with humor and human communication and how far you can go with another. He was not from here—not originally, anyway—and they say things differently in other places. They have a different sense of humor. I knew that from my own grandparents who communicated in a different language, even though the words came out in a language that sounded much like English. He'd had a hard life. How could I know that? *Had* he? Maybe he'd had a fantastic life. But then why do you shut yourself away? When have we had enough? Enough pleasure. Enough pain. These were not questions I could formulate sufficiently to bring to anyone I knew. Questions like these would make my mother worry. They would make Richie Koestler and Donny Eisenstadt laugh. Kids on the playground already taunted me for asking *heavy questions*. Doc, they called me. "Just punch the damn ball, Doc" was a common response to my questions about life, death, existence, and music. As in…

"Did you know that The Beatles use perfect-fifth harmonies in 'She Loves You' and 'I Wanna Hold Your Hand'? No one has done that since hillbilly music. And, before that—"

"Hey, Doc. Just punch the damn ball."

The only place I could go was to the piano. Hopefully I would find answers there. The piano spoke to me and I understood it. When my mother was around I would practice my Kabalevsky Sonatina dutifully, if without inspiration. But, left alone, I could talk to the piano and it would talk back to me. It never told me to be quiet, keep my thoughts to myself, though it did tell me when I was not expressing myself as well as possible, and if I listened closely it showed me how to say what I meant.

I could close my eyes and pick out four or six notes—preferably sets of mismatched perfect fourths and fifths—and play them again and again *and again*. Five ten twenty minutes long. Louder softer faster slower *staccato legato sostenuto*…. I would play paradiddles and flams. I would play two against one and three against two. I would rest my head on the piano's beam and let the sound pour straight into my skull. Make my body one with the wood and the strings. The longer I played, the sharper the overtones struck, the deeper the undertones reached. With the lights out and my eyes closed, the angels were welcome into the room and they sat with me, sang along with me, as I played. Sometimes we would laugh together. Sometimes they brought intense sadness. They never brought answers but I always went to bed knowing we'd had an important talk.

{

MY PIANO TEACHER was a tiny, elderly woman who loved to laugh. Her hair was dyed the color of a copper pot and she had wrestled it to the best of her ability into a messy knot on the top of her head. She wore rows of wooden beads circled and recircled around her skinny neck. Her hands were withered and the veins and tendons protruded through the skin. Whenever I came into her house she would shout *"Darling!"* and give me a hug. She wore old lady's perfume that made her smell like some puffy flower, but it suited her.

She lived in a grand apartment in the East Sixties filled with ancient furniture. At the far end of her living room stood two nine-foot concert grand pianos nestled into each other's curves. The whole place smelled faintly of talcum powder.

She took my hands and looked at me. "Have you grown again?"

I smiled. "Lily, you saw me last week."

She giggled and waved the idea away. "No. I'm the one who's shrinking." She went into her kitchen and came out a minute later with a glass of Coca-Cola. "Don't tell your mother."

"Don't worry. I won't."

She took her place next to my piano stool. "So, let me hear my favorite underachiever."

I wanted to argue. I wanted to tell her I had practiced

enough. That I had finally decided to make the most of my musical potential.

I sat down and started to play the Kabalevsky.

"Scales, Michael, please. Make an old lady happy and warm up a little, first."

I hated scales.

"D Major, please."

I sighed as quietly as I could and played scales. One against one. Two against one. Three against one. Three against two…

"More?"

"Yes, please. And this time with your eyes closed. Or otherwise look at the ceiling. When are you going to start trusting your fingers?"

I fought through the scales, trying again to think of ways to make them more fun, but I could not. I was chewing through sawdust. Finally, at her nod, I was able to move on to my study and, at once, wondered what my hurry had been. I wasn't at all prepared and felt embarrassed to show her that. The music I made sounded nothing like music. I was trudging through a pool of nuts and bolts, ball bearings, and brass tacks. The music itself reminded me of a poster my Social Studies teacher had shown us—Soviet workers with rectangular Soviet heads, waving rectangular Soviet flags. There was no softness or warmth. It was too important. But in my rendition, I wasn't even able to show that.

I finally made it to the end and sighed out loud. I stared at my knees.

Now it was her turn to sigh. She dropped her head and pinched the bridge of her nose. "*Wow*." There was a mirthless giggle in there. "I thought I might have to send out a search party."

I could not bear to look at her. For someone who, in her eyes, could do no wrong, I was pushing the limits.

"Michael, what are we going to do with you? You're the worst wonderful musician I've ever known."

I could only stare at the keyboard, which had failed me, and which I had failed.

"I *hate* this piece." I wanted to gasp or clasp my hand over my mouth, but boys didn't do that. I looked to see her response.

There was the tiniest smile in one corner of her mouth. "Well, in all fairness, you're not making it very interesting… for you, for me, or anyone else."

Make it interesting?

"Shove over."

She had to reach up to hit the keys. The veins in her hands protruded even further through the parchment of her skin, but the sound that came out surprised me. She played twice as loud as I. All of a sudden the music was angry and moody. Then brave. Then sad. And, finally, triumphant.

I wanted to ask her how she had done that. I wanted to ask her why she didn't perform for great audiences. I wanted to tell her that I could never do what she had just done. I felt inspired. I felt hopeless.

"And, by the way, you don't really think you'll make me believe you're reading. You memorized this thing a long time ago. Turning the pages in more or less the right places won't help either of us. We both know you can memorize anything. But you have *got* to learn how to read."

"I can read." The words did not sound particularly convincing as they came out.

"You know what I mean. I want you to sit down to a new piece of music and just sight-read it. Just play it off first time." She swiveled around and looked at me. "So? What now?"

My mind raced. I had always imagined myself making beautiful music. I loved nothing more than the sound of getting it just right. Nothing matched that pleasure. I arrived at an impossible solution.

"Give me something *hard* to play."

"Oh, like that's gonna help."

"Well… yeah. It'll make me read. Maybe it'll make me more… I don't know… More interested." What was the word my mother liked to use? "More *motivated*."

I could see her considering the idea. "OK, what do you suggest?"

"*Bach.*" I was nearly shouting.

"Michael, we've already been that route. You didn't have much more luck—"

"Not one of his *teaching* pieces. Not something for learning. You know. A beautiful piece."

"A performance piece."

"A *performance* piece." The words excited me.

She examined my face. "Something hard?" She thought for a moment, then walked over to her shelves of sheet music. Books, folders, mimeographs, and Photostats were stacked at every angle, but she knew where everything was. With her back to me she said, "You like Bach, right?"

"Well, yeah. Just as long as it's not…"

"Pedantic?"

"Uhm… yeah." I would look it up when I got home.

She came back with a thin booklet of sheet music.

Johan Sebastian Bach
Harpsichord Concerto No. 5 in F Minor
BWV 1056 — II: *Largo*

I opened it and tried not to gasp. Four flats? What had I done?

She saw my face and chuckled. "Don't worry. You'll start with the simpler part."

"No." The sound of my voice surprised me. *"I'll* play the hard part." In fact, I wanted to give in, but granting her offer to make it easy would mean my defeat.

For a moment, I didn't know if she was going to hug me or smack me. She sighed.

"Michael, it's only simpler because it has fewer notes to play. But, I promise you, it is *not* easier. That's how we're gonna do this."

Clearly I did not look happy.

"Don't worry. It'll be hard enough, I promise. I've given you the solo part to play." She pointed at this piano's twin with her chin. "I'll play the orchestral part. Anyway, it's time we did some ensemble playing." She locked her eyes on me. "But listen. No screwing around. You *learn* this."

I was struck with fear. I had committed myself. I wanted to run away. But to let her down would mean letting myself down.

Her face softened. "I tell you what. Let me play you a version so you know what to expect." She walked over to her record collection. She had at least as many records as Mr. Kreitz but hers were in no particular order. They were piled on the floor, or sideways on top of the original neat rows on her shelves. Miraculously, again, she found it in seconds.

The music that reached out from the hi-fi was new to me. At once I understood. The notes were not difficult, but this was going to be a difficult piece to make beautiful—impossible to make as beautiful as this.

After just two measures the room grew dark. It was a summer evening. The air cooled and the sun set. I lay on the beach at the lake. I smelled the water. A bird hissed past. Fish disturbed the surface. Footsteps on pine needles. I saw a star-filled sky and each star was its own note. The lake reflected the night. There were insects buzzing. Crickets singing. Miniature waves lapped against the sand. The sand was cool. The pines behind me breathed in time. Every note, every phrase, was in the perfect place. The music of the spheres. The harmony of the world.

Three minutes later, the music swelled, inhaled deeply, and—*what?*

"That can't be the end. There must be more. That chord is saying, *there's more.*"

"That's right. A concerto has three movements. It goes fast-slow-fast. This is the slow movement. The second movement. That's a dominant chord at the end. It says, *here comes the final part.* If you do well, we can do the rest. But this is the easiest and, I think, the most beautiful part."

"It's one of the most beautiful things I've ever heard."

"*Good*, darling." She reached up, pinched my cheek gently, rested her hand on my shoulder, and smiled. "Then you'll work hard." She examined my face. "OK, what's up?"

"Lily, I don't know where to begin."

She seemed interested by my remark. "You mean besides the beginning."

"Well, the notes aren't hard. Not really. But the piece is hard. I don't even know how to say it."

"Can you give me a for instance?"

I closed my eyes and listened back. "Sometimes the pianist is playing completely off the beat, completely out of time, but it's perfect. How can that be?"

She smiled and thought a moment. "Come here." She opened up the sheet music on the piano lectern, took a pencil, and pointed at white space—a big gap—between the notes on the page.

"What's that?" she asked.

I looked at her a little dimly, I think. Was this a trick question?

"What would you call that?" she repeated.

"It… You're not pointing at anything." I watched the muscles of her face looking for a sign, for a change. "It's paper?"

She closed her eyes and sighed. "Michael, please. Not the paper. What's *on* the paper?"

"Well, nothing."

This time, she clearly tried to repress another sigh. She rocked her head to one side. "OK, we're getting closer. It's *something* like nothing, I suppose. What's another name for nothing?"

I felt myself falling. What was I missing?

"Uhm… Space?"

"OK. Good. That's one word for it."

"Lily, I don't know what you want me to say. I'm not seeing what you want me to see."

"Music, Michael. It's *music*."

Again I had nothing to hold onto. The piano bench under me offered no support. I tried to keep my voice calm. "It… looks to me like you're pointing in between the notes. In between the music."

Now her smile was genuine. "And the space in between the notes *isn't* music?"

I felt comforted by the smile. I had long decided that I no longer required the approval of adults. But that meant I could only be letting myself down.

≀

TIME CHANGED. It expanded in the daylight hours and contracted at night. I could feel time stroking across my body with the summer air. It was in the beat of the music on the radio. In the tick of the wind-up alarm clock next to my bed. In the drip of the kitchen faucet. It tapped me on the shoulder at unexpected moments.

I continued to play punchball with my friends. I continued to play piano. I made deliveries at the delicatessen on my appointed days. So what was different? There were questions now. The Hermit had asked questions that I could not answer. Not earth-shaking questions. Not *is-the-world-coming-to-an-end* questions. But as I reconstructed our conversation, as I had done every day since our meeting, I realized I could not really remember what he had asked. Had he asked me if I loved music? If I wanted to be a musician? Maybe he had asked me *why* I loved music so much. I could not remember. Somewhere, as time continued to flex and deform, his questions commingled with my own.

The week did not so much roll around as scrape and grind until it reached the moment when the order for pot roast came in as it had a week before.

Mr. Kahanah hung up the phone. He turned to me.

"It's Mister Kreitz with the pot roast again. Do you mind bringing it over to him?"

"Who?"

"You know. The Hermit I called him."

Mrs. Kahanah had just walked in from the back room.

"Sherman, *please*. That's not a nice thing to say." She turned to me and shook her head. "That's not a nice thing to say about a person."

The roll of his eyes said *Do I care?*

"He has a name." Mrs. Kahanah sounded a little like my third grade teacher as she spoke each syllable. "Eugene Kreitz."

Mr. Kahanah waited patiently until she finished. "Anyway, do you mind bringing it over? It's the end of your shift. You could do it on your way home."

"Why would I mind?"

"Well, you know. You might have found him a little... weird or something."

"He's a perfectly nice man," she broke in. "He's a little lonely, that's all."

I put on my best smile and tried to look at the both of them. "It's fine. We talked for a minute. About music."

"Oh, yeah," Mr. Kahanah examined his memory. "He was a musician or something."

I nodded. "A violinist."

They both turned to me in surprise.

"You talked with him?"

"Oh... not long or anything." I felt the need to clear myself of some aberrant behavior. "Just for a few minutes. But I like music and he was in the mood to talk. Anyway, it was the end of my shift. So..."

"Isn't that nice?" Mrs. Kahanah burst out. "Didn't I tell you? *This is such a nice boy.*"

As I mounted my bike, I wondered for a moment just what I was doing. I had thought all week about seeing the Hermit again, but why? I had wanted to talk to him so much—but about what? Did I still want to speak to him? What had we spoken about the first time? What made this encounter so urgent? I still wanted to talk to him. I just didn't have anything to say.

I brought the wrapped pot roast to his door again and tapped the knocker four times in honor of Beethoven, or my father, or both, or neither.

I had hardly finished knocking when I heard the deadbolt flip over. The door opened an inch and I could see one eye peering through. The door then opened rapidly. This time he gave me a big smile.

"Ah, the young musician. I hoped it would be you."

I was at a loss for words. Why would he want to see me? I did my best to mumble a greeting and followed him into the living room. Nothing had changed. Even the dust in the air appeared to be in the same place. He smiled again as he took the package from me and brought it to the kitchen. For a moment, I was alone in the living room. This time, though, I found a neutral spot away from the piano and the record collection.

He called from the kitchen. "Michael, was it?"

"That's right."

"I thought about your question. About why I have a piano—a pretty nice one, all in all—if I don't tune it or use it. So I had it tuned."

I knew what was coming. I hadn't practiced. I hadn't prepared. I hadn't taken him seriously. I hadn't even said

I would play. But the request was on its way. "Comin'
Thro' the Rye"? "Love Me Do"? This was useless. It had
to be classical. Something I knew. It didn't matter if I
had played it to death.

"So would you mind playing something for me?"

I shrugged. Why didn't I just say no?

"It's been so long since I've heard live music." He
came in to the room and saw my face. "I'm sorry, do you
need to get back to work?"

Why didn't I lie?

"Sure. I can play something." I had already decided
what to play.

His face shone with delight. I rarely got this kind of
reception.

"Should I wash my hands first? My mom always
makes me wash my hands."

"She does? That sounds pretty serious."

"Well, she likes to keep the piano clean and she says
the warm water relaxes your muscles."

"Well, I think your mother sounds very sensible."

I shrugged.

"So you'll play something?"

I always had a piece ready. The request came on some
kind of regular basis. Grownups didn't ask other
grownups to play, but they did ask kids. That was
allowed for some reason. I didn't like it but I knew I had
to be prepared for it. At what age would people stop
asking me to play? So, for a few minutes—not so often,
every few months—I would become Michael, the piano-
playing monkey, just to please the adults. And, hopefully,
to stop them from asking again.

I sat down and, without even breathing, I launched into Bach's Prelude No. 1 in C Major. It was easy. It had some nice chord progressions in it. I could play it in my sleep. I may have even been asleep while I was playing it.

I finished and stared at the keyboard. I felt nothing. I had done my duty.

"What's wrong? What is it?" he said.

I realized I was frowning and he had seen it.

"Well, the piano's still out of tune."

I heard him draw breath. "Now that's what I call an ear. You can hear that?"

"Well…" I shrugged again. "It's out of tune. I mean, it's not as bad as it *was*. It's *much* better than…" I was only making it worse.

"You're right, of course. The piano hasn't been tuned in so long that the strings have bounced."

"They what?"

"Strings have a kind of memory. They want to go back to their old tuning. It needs a second tuning. In fact the piano tuner said it would need that."

"I'm sorry. I shouldn't have said that."

"Not to worry." He smiled. "But then I have a request. Next time, would you play something you *like* to play?"

Was it that obvious?

"Do you like Rock and Roll Music?" He pronounced the *and*.

I suppressed my smile. The words sounded ridiculous coming out of this old man's mouth. "Do you like… uhm… Elvis Presley?"

Jesus, he really was out of touch.

"Well, not really. He's kind of old-fashioned."

"So what do you listen to when you don't have to please old people?"

"I like The Beatles and The Rolling Stones and people like that."

"Ah, they're the *cool* ones these days?"

Even that sounded stupid coming from him. I shrugged one shoulder and nodded. I had mastered my smile muscles. I actually felt for him. He was trying his best.

"Is their music—how shall I call it—rebellious?"

"I guess so. Old people… well, my mother just says it's a bunch of noise."

"Can you play something for me so I can hear what it sounds like. It's true. I do tend to change the radio station when it comes on. But, maybe you can teach me about it."

The thought of teaching *him* something seemed strange to me. I liked to think of myself as worldly wise. I was nearly as tall as he. I was physically fit. He was small and hunched over. And now, in his presence, I felt tiny. I turned around to face the piano and thought for a moment. I wanted to play, "A Hard Day's Night" because I wanted him to hear all the complexity of the opening chord but, very simply, I could not. I hesitated.

"Too hard to play?"

I could not see his face. Was he looking over my shoulder? I imagined he was making fun of me.

"I play most of this stuff on the guitar."

"So, you play guitar, too." He sounded genuinely impressed. "This I didn't know. But is there nothing that you can translate from that stringed instrument to this one?"

How could these both be stringed instruments? Of course they weren't. He was teasing me. Why all this provocation? More important, why couldn't I beat him at his own game? Beat him at his own challenge. Shock him with the shocking music of my generation. There must be something I could play. Could I play "House of the Rising Sun"? I couldn't sing that low. "I Wanna Hold Your Hand"? No, you needed harmony for that. And, playing on the piano and singing was complicated enough. All of a sudden, the songs I loved sounded stupid in front of this old man. How could it be that "Do Wah Diddy" suddenly sounded like mindless babble when, until this moment, it had only filled me with joy to shout the lyrics at the radio together with my friends? I wanted to hang my music in his face and say *smell that why don't you*. So, why this need for him to respect me?

I chose "You Really Got Me" by The Kinks. One voice, mostly. Simple chords. Not too many mistakes, I hoped. He stood behind me and watched my hands. I could almost hear him raising his eyebrows in surprise. I rested my hands on the keyboard and mimicked some of the chords I would have to play.

"G Major?"

I struggled for a moment about what to say. "A lot of guitar songs are in E." I put a smile in my voice. "But then I'd have to play B-seven and I can't do that on the piano without getting it wrong."

He chuckled warmly. "Accidental accidents."

"Well, I can play it on the guitar, no problem." *So*

why not on the piano?

I played the opening measures and he listened closely. He seemed even to stop breathing for a moment. I found it miserably hard to sing without messing up the chords. What had Ray Davis done? What was he doing to me? He was put-*ting* all the ac-*cents* on the wrongs syl-*lab*-les. How could he get away with that?

I stuttered out the words. I missed the entrance on the fourth measure entirely. After a while, I gave up.

He straightened up. "I see." He thought for a second. "One-two-five chord structure. Lots of elision. Some syncopation. Common time. This is rebellious music?"

"Well, my mom thinks so. She's always telling me to turn it down."

"So maybe it's rebellious because it's loud?"

"Well, I still don't think she'd like the music if I played it softer."

"Why not?"

In fact, I did not know. I hadn't had to explain that to anyone before. I resented having to explain it to anyone.

"Maybe I should bring the record around."

He nodded. "You could do that, but I'd like to know why you think it's rebellious. Oh, dear, I've annoyed you. I'm not your teacher. And the last thing you want is to get homework from some old man."

"Oh, it's not that." (Of course it was.) "It's just so obvious to *me* why Rock music—Rock 'n' Roll, I mean—is crazy. It makes you want to jump up and down and shout. I feel… It's hard to explain. I feel like I'm doing something bad—something I shouldn't be doing—when I listen to it."

I had to smile. I had never thought of that before.

"Well, then." Now it was his turn to shrug. "Maybe *that's* what makes it rebellious. It's not the chord progression or the syncopation. It's the feeling *behind* the music that counts, not the notes. The notes are almost secondary." He thought about that. "Haven't you ever noticed that, when one of your friends plays the very same song that you've heard on the radio, you get a different feeling? Why would that be? Sure he might be a little less… well, less *competent* at his instrument, but there's something else, isn't there?"

How could he know this? He didn't even like Rock music. I wasn't sure if he was waiting for an answer so I nodded to keep him talking.

"Otherwise we could build machines that made music." He laughed. "And get rid of all those annoying musicians. But it's the *feeling* that we want. Music—the person *and* the instrument *and* that which is written down—all create the vehicle. Don't get me wrong. It's the *greatest* vehicle. But what we are creating is *feeling*. And, speaking of jumping up and down, there are some pretty crazy stories about the premiere of Beethoven's Ninth Symphony. So it didn't just start with Rock and Roll."

We were both silent for our own reasons. He shook himself awake.

"So, who are you studying?"

"Sorry?"

"What music, *classical* music, are you practicing?"

"*Oh.* Kabalevsky."

"Ah, Comrade Kabalevsky." He pronounced

Kabalevsky in a way I could not.

"Comrade? Do you know him?"

He chuckled. "Not exactly. Not *that* kind of comrade, anyway. But, a long time ago, we knew many of the same people." His eyes came back into the room from far away. "May I hear you play it?"

"*No.*" I nearly shouted. "I mean… I'm not any good at it. I mean… I've only just started on it," I lied.

"Ah, of course. Well, I'm impressed that you have the maturity to set standards. You won't just play anything for anyone."

I felt myself blush and I tried to laugh it away. "Well, I'll try to get it… up to standard."

"Hey I have an idea. Would you join me for lunch one afternoon? We could continue our talks without your having to run back to the delicatessen."

Why would I want to spend my free time with this guy? I already saw him more often than I visited with my own grandmother.

I shrugged. "I dunno. I have the delivery job and I like to go to the playground on the weekends."

"Ah… OK. Of course. I just thought, if you didn't have anything else to do, you could keep me company and I could help you with your music. A silly idea. All the music I hear these days is through speakers."

"Why don't you go to a concert? My mother always says she could never live outside of New York because she would have to leave Carnegie Hall and Lincoln Center behind."

He lost his smile.

"I can't do that."

I just stared at him. I had heard of people who were afraid of going outside but I had never seen it up close.

"Don't you… do you ever go to the grocery store… or stuff?"

"Oh, yes. I can do that. That's not it."

I watched him closely. His face had changed. He wasn't sad. Not exactly angry. Rather, his face was drained of all expression. He stared out the window and his breathing had become very quiet. It felt like a long time before he spoke.

He changed his face to a smile.

"Come to lunch and I'll try to explain."

ʔ

I ARRIVED HOME to find my brother Simon lying on the couch reading *Nine Stories* by J.D. Salinger. His long legs dangled over one end of our little two-seater. He looked up at me, no real expression in his eyes, and returned to his book. He wasn't home much. I wasn't surprised when he was gone, wasn't surprised when he was home.

"I'm going play some piano."

He didn't look up. "Sure. OK."

I decided to practice "You Really Got Me." My mother wasn't back from school, yet, so I could sing along. I didn't care if Simon heard. Anyway, he didn't hear anything when he was caught up in a book.

I had no idea if my voice was good or not, but that didn't seem very important at this moment. I just wanted to get it right. The chords, the melody—it all had to mesh. What was so hard about playing one rhythm and singing another? Was that what made the music rebellious? Maybe it only had to do with the fact that it wasn't the music of my mother's youth. Had Benny Goodman made the music of the devil in his time? I found that hard to believe. But that was what they had called Elvis's music just a decade ago. Now it just seemed harmless. What did teenagers listen to in the time of Beethoven?

I realized I was practicing the wrong thing.

I pulled out my *Twentieth-Century Piano, Part II* from under my mother's stack of music and it fell open to the Kabalevsky. I shouted behind me.

"Simon, I could be practicing for a while."

He didn't respond.

I'm going to practice this, in fact, until I don't make a single mistake with the notes. Only then can I start thinking about the feeling behind them.

Again, time changed shape—and sound with it. The space surrounding the piano absorbed all light and sound inward and out—absorbing me. There was just enough air to breathe, but no excess. There was no smell, but touch increased. The piano keys reached into my fingers. The pedals pushed against my feet. I would sustain bodily damage if I tried to remove myself from the instrument. A hundred miles away, a dog barked. My brother disappeared from the adjoining room. Light shone only on my sheet music. Somewhere in the distance, a door slammed. A voice shouted, *Hello?* A dark form moved around me.

"Wow, I don't think I've ever heard you take this piece so slowly."

I startled awake. "God, you scared me."

My mother was leaning one elbow on the piano. "Now that's what I call concentration. By all means, don't stop." She walked behind me and kissed me on the top of my head. I had to stop myself from pushing her away. How could she not feel this force field around me?

A minute later, she returned to the piano.

"*Hey, you.* I've been calling you to come to dinner."

"I'm not hungry."

She shrugged. "Get it while it's hot. And while I never thought I'd hear myself speak these words, I think it's probably time to stop. You'll burn yourself out. There's also such a thing as too much practice."

I considered the idea and then realized my hands were aching.

I crossed the living room to the dinner table to find my mother and brother already eating.

"There you are."

"He's been at it for hours," my brother said.

I looked at them. They appeared to be waiting for some kind of explanation.

"Lily won't let me move on to another piece until I get this one right." Sometimes lies were just easier and faster.

My mother smiled. "Well, thank goodness for Lily."

They seemed appeased by the explanation and continued their conversation. My mother talked about her day's teaching. My brother talked about his college courses. But the music continued to play in my head. Dessert was a piece of fruit and a Hershey Bar divided three ways. My mother watched me.

"You OK? You're awfully quiet. Even for you."

"Sorry. I probably just practiced too much. I've got the music stuck in my head."

"Hey, don't get me wrong. I'm thrilled to see you taking this so seriously."

Was that approval or criticism in disguise? I wasn't sure I cared. I didn't say anything.

We finished dinner. My brother and I cleared the

table. He scraped the dishes. I wiped down the table, filled the sink with hot water and two squeezes of dish soap and Simon laid the dishes in to soak. My mother would wash them later. But the music would not stop.

"Wanna watch a movie on TV?" It was Simon, somewhere faraway.

"What?"

"A movie. *East of Eden*. James Dean?"

"Nah, you go ahead."

My hands were exhausted, my head was ringing, but I could not stop. It would not stop and I didn't want it to. I took the sheet music to my bedroom, I lay on my bed and stared at the notes, the chords, and the phrases until I fell asleep.

{

I WAS EATING my bowl of Cheerios and milk (with what my mother referred to as "a disgusting amount of sugar") when the doorbell rang. No one else seemed to be around so I answered the door intercom. It was Jack, the columnist from the Sunday brunch group.

"I don't think my mom's here. She gives lessons on Saturday mornings."

"Nah, I came for you. I got tickets for the ball game. Wanna go?"

I glanced over at the piano.

"Now?"

"Whyn't you let me in?"

I buzzed the door open. Even pressing on the button made my hand hurt. How long had I played yesterday? I had planned on practicing again and had to wonder if I really could. I opened the door to our apartment, slid the welcome mat under the door with my foot so the wind wouldn't close it again, and then went back to my cereal. A minute later, the door opened and shut. Jack came in and sat down next to me. He had a bright smile on his face. It was clear he had been awake for hours. He was wearing a pressed button-down, short-sleeve Paisley shirt. His graying hair was slicked back and his mustache was neatly trimmed. Some days he wore a clip-on bowtie.

Today his shirt was open at the neck. I got a faint whiff of Aqua Velva. He inspected me briefly.

"You just crawl out of bed, Tiger? Ah, to be a teenager, again."

I looked down and realized I still had pajama-bottoms and a tee-shirt on. The TV, now on the dining table, was playing a Bugs Bunny cartoon.

"You mind if I turn that down?"

"It's OK, just turn it off."

"So, you keeping busy?"

"Yeah, I guess. I'm making deliveries at the deli and trying to keep the piano going."

He smiled and nodded. "Good. Good." He thought for a moment. "So… any thoughts about joining me for the ball game?"

"Oh, right. Where is it?"

A wide smile grew across his face. "The Cathedral."

"What? You got Yankees tickets on a weekend?"

He sat back and folded his hands behind his head. "You just gotta know the right people." He smiled. "Hey, if you're gonna come with, you need to get dressed so we can go."

The thought of a Yankees game on a beautiful day like this was irresistible. That and my hands hurt too much to practice, so the choice was obvious. I threw on my clothes—lying on the floor from the day before— and we were heading for the Christopher Street station inside of ten minutes.

The air was hot but a sweet-smelling breeze pushed us down the street. The piano part to "Summer in the City" played in my head.

My mother had instructed me to show an interest in adults. "So… how're you?"

"Oh, you know. The *Empire Review* keeps me off the streets. No rest for the wicked."

"Do you have like a regular job with them?"

"Not really. Sort of. We call it a gentlemen's agreement. I write an article about the city—something going on in the city. If they like it, they pay me and ask for another one. After twenty years, I guess we each know what the other one wants. It works pretty good." He looked at me and laughed. "At age thirteen, I doubt you can imagine doing *anything* for twenty years."

Except that I could.

"Well, but, do you like it?"

Jack had to think about that one for a moment. "Well, I'm not sure *like* is really the right word. I *have to* write. If I don't, I'll go nuts. I see things. I hear things. I *know* things. And I have to write them down. And, preferably, in a way that looks and reads great. If I don't, my fingers get… what's the word… itchy. My whole *brain* gets itchy."

"So, if you didn't write…"

"…I'd go nuts."

"But couldn't you get a job doing something else and just write for fun?"

"Nope, that's not happenin'. How can I explain it?" He had to stop walking to say this correctly. "I basically have to write all the time. The only way to do that is to write *well*. If I didn't write well, I'd have to get a job doing something else. *Then* I'd go nuts. So I have to be the best writer I can possibly be. It wasn't really my idea, or my wish, to be a writer—to *achieve* as a writer. It was only when I realized that, to be able to keep writing, I had to be the best damn writer I knew how to be." He examined my face. "Does that make any sense?"

I nodded again.

"There are folks out there who like to write. They like to—I dunno—play guitar. They think anthropology is pretty neat. Or they're perfectly happy working in a gas station. I don't know whether to envy people like that or pity them. They can go and do any kind of job. Then they can come home and do something else. So they're free, but there's no passion. You can't be a professional writer—or you *shouldn't* be one—unless it's *all* you want to be. Unless it's all you *can* do." He looked closer at me. "Mike, are you all right?"

"Yeah… no, I'm fine. I just never heard anyone say that before."

He watched me. "The music? Really? The way I understand it, your mom's always bitchin' at you to practice."

I forced a laugh. "Yeah, I guess, I don't want to practice. I just want to know how to play already."

Jack laughed out loud. "Oh, yeah. That one. You're what, twelve?"

"Thirteen."

"Well, if you're telling the truth, that's gonna have to change. *You're* gonna have to change."

I cringed. "It sounds awful."

He giggled. "Oh, you get used to it."

"How can it be nice if you can't get away from that feeling?"

"Well, I guess it becomes a way of life. You give in to it. Writing is more than what I do. It's what I am. I'm a writer. I'm not just someone who likes to write."

There was that feeling again.

"It's not all that bad. I called it giving in. It's more like happy surrender." He checked my face again. "I tell you what. Let's not think about it too much right now. I may be a writer, but I also wanna be in time for the ball game. So can we keep walking?"

"Oh… yeah." We walked in silence for a moment. "Hey, I didn't even ask you who they're playing."

This time his smile was slightly wicked. "The Senators."

I wrinkled my nose. "*No*. The Yanks are gonna smash them!"

"Yeah." He giggled like a little kid. "It's gonna be great."

❧

THE GAME WAS GREAT. Yankee Stadium was always breezy, at least up in the cheap seats. And, under the shade of the eaves, it wasn't hot at all.

Everyone was in a good mood. Lots of chatter and laughter among strangers.

I watched Jack taking in the whole scene. Players from both teams were out on the field warming up—stretching, playing catch, jogging around the field. Two players went over to members of the other team to greet them, shaking their hands, laughing, and joking.

"If there *is* a heaven—something I seriously doubt, by the way—I imagine it looks a little like this." He thought a moment, grabbed a tiny notepad and pen from his breast pocket, flipped the sorely curled pages back to find a clean one, and started writing. "That's going in my next column."

There *was* something magical about leaving the heat and dust of the city and finding ourselves amid all this green, rather like passing through to a secret world. The flags above the outfield fence were flapping for joy. The stadium organ was playing "The Sidewalks of New York."

I listened and thought for a moment. "Isn't that a

funny job to have?"

"Being a writer?"

"Sorry, no, the organ player at a baseball stadium."

He looked up at the grass and listened. I realized he hadn't heard it until this moment. How could you *not* hear music?

He smiled. "Guess so. Never really thought about it. It's not a job a lot of people have." He waved the back of his hand over the field. "This is what I was talking about. Here's a guy who's got to play, no matter what. He can't not play."

I thought about that and listened closely. It was clear the organist was not playing from sheet music. Each phrase had a few different notes that were there just to make the song interesting. In any case he was very good and I imagined he was having fun. Or otherwise he was bored to death at having played this song for the nine-thousandth time and was just trying to entertain himself.

The music did a neat segue into a song I didn't know. It sounded upbeat and jazzy.

Jack laughed. He was clearly listening more closely, now. "That's 'Take The "A" Train.' He's going out on a limb with this one." I looked at him for explanation and he pointed at the seats past the outfield. "I doubt the Bleacher Bums are real jazz lovers."

How could anyone not like this? It was happy music. It took lots of unexpected turns. It was fun to listen to.

"What do you think he does when he's not playing here?"

He shrugged. "Playing piano in a jazz club on Fifty-Second Street, maybe."

The music took another turn.

"Hey, I know this!" I said. "It's the song from 'The Danny Thomas Show'."

Jack smiled. "It's actually an old Irish folk tune called 'Danny Boy.' No, it has another name, but people call it 'Danny Boy'."

"It is?" It was clear to me, anyway, that the organist had heard the TV sitcom version because he was playing it almost note for note. Who'd had the idea to change an Irish tune into a Big Band piece? I thought about all the talent that went into TV music. "The Dick van Dyke Show" was a bouncy Big Band tune that moved with the action on the screen. "I Dream of Jeannie" was actually two songs in perfect counterpoint. "My Three Sons" also had two tunes at once, and one of them was the children's piano piece "Chopsticks" played three-over-two. So many talented musicians. Was there room for all of them? Where would they all fit?

Where would I fit?

{

I SAT THINKING to myself on the subway home from the baseball game. Jack was scribbling away in his little pad again. I guessed he'd had a good idea for a story. And anyway, the old subway—with its windows wide open in the summer heat—made it impossible to have any real conversation. From our left, a large Black man, a blind man, came through the door from the adjacent subway car. He had a large saxophone hung around his neck. He steadied himself against the pole at the end of car and, with his other hand, slid the connecting door shut behind him. He then put the instrument's mouthpiece to his lips and started playing as he walked through the car. There was a tin cup tied to the lowest bend of his instrument and, as he walked, a few people dropped a few coins into the cup. When he heard the coins land he would turn vaguely in the direction of the sound and nod in thanks. Sometimes he nodded in the wrong direction. Sometimes he just nodded straight ahead of him. I had seen him lots of times before so his presence was not a surprise. I wondered how long he had actually been doing this. I wondered if he could really make a living this way, just on a bunch of coins. The hours it took from his day couldn't allow him to do any other work.

His eyes were purplish gray all the way around—he didn't seem to have any whites to his eyes—and they stared out at nothing. Even so, he always managed to walk a perfectly straight line down the middle of the subway car and knew exactly where every pole was. He never lost his balance, even as the subway jerked and swayed on its path, and he knew exactly how long the subway car was.

The subway was so noisy that I could barely hear anything he was playing, even when he walked straight past me. Without looking up, Jack reached into his pocket, rummaged around, and dropped fifteen cents into the tin cup as he passed. The Black man turned in Jack's direction and nodded. Simon had once explained to me that the saxophone he was playing was called a tenor, which was why it was so large and sounded so deep. This particular example looked old and sad. It was dented and bore the heavy tarnish of an instrument that had not seen proper care.

Close up, I could say the same of his clothes. They were not dirty and he did not appear at all unsanitary. But neither did he look tidily dressed and well looked after.

My mother had instructed me never to stare at anyone who looked different in any way, whether because of physical restriction or religious statement. But I could stare at this blind, Black, saxophone-playing wanderer, and I liked to because I had the feeling he knew something I didn't. Each time I saw him. I examined his face for a sign. Was he happy? Was he unhappy? Did he like this job? I imagined he could have chosen to do or be something else, but was even that true?

He reached the end of the subway car and turned around to finish what he was playing. For a moment, I could hear just a swatch of a tune. And, as tunes so often do, it reminded me of another tune, one that my mother sang to me when I was little, especially when I had a cold.

Id aid godda raid doe bore, doe bore
Id aid godda raid doe bore
How idda heck cad I wash by deck
If id aid godda raid doe bore?

On other nights she liked to sing a little ditty and poke me gently in the ribs with each note. Years later, I realized it was not a lullaby at all, but the second movement of Haydn's "Surprise" Symphony which takes a comic turn after sixteen measures.

When had she stopped singing to me? Had I given her some signal to indicate that I was now too old for that? Had she decided that I was old enough to put myself to bed? Had she said to me, *I won't be tucking you in as of tonight*? Do parents do that?

{

I NEVER FORGOT how Lily had played the Kabalevsky sonatina. She had filled it with emotion. She gave it colors and smells. She made it sound foreign. I had been trying to make it sound familiar.

Now that I had all the notes in the right place, I didn't know whether to work out the fine points with Lily before taking it to Mr. Kreitz or to clean it up with him in preparation for my lesson. Finally, after even more practice and a lot of worry, I realized that everything I did in music—everything I ever would do in music— would be for him. Lily was my teacher, but that's all she was.

In between sips of my ritual, secret glass of soda, I explained to Lily that I had decided to give the Kabalevsky one more try before moving on to the Bach. It didn't seem quite right, I said. I had learned so much from hearing her play it. She thought about that for a moment and nodded. I was relieved at how easily she had taken the lie. She had allowed me to move on to another piece, but there was still Mr. Kreitz. He still wanted to hear it. I could have said no, but I didn't. I couldn't.

I played a few scales to please her and then launched straight in. I thought about the timing, the staccatos and legatos, the fortes and the pianos. I watched my fingering. I didn't listen to the music very closely but that didn't seem quite as important right now. I just had to make sure that the harmonies and melodies were in balance. But I didn't dare to get lost in the music. There was too much to think about.

I finished and realized I felt exhausted, but I felt pretty sure had gotten it right.

Lily stirred in her seat. I could feel her looking at me but I didn't dare to look at her. There was a long silence. Finally I heard her breathe in.

"OK, who are you and what have you done with Michael?"

All I could do was stare at the piano keys. I hoped I wasn't blushing.

"Mike, can you please tell me what happened? You couldn't play this piece for beans. You hated it. You said you didn't even want to play it anymore."

"I didn't. I don't. I dunno. I just decided it was time to start practicing."

She giggled. "So this was the only way to be well and truly done with it?"

I nodded but it was better not to look at her. That wasn't the reason, of course, and I could tell she knew it.

She stood up, which made her only marginally taller than me sitting down. She hugged me around the neck, kissed me loudly on the side of the head, and then wiped the spot hard with her thumb.

"OK, we're done for the day."

"Huh? Lily, we still have a half hour."

She tilted her head to one side. "Far as I can tell, we're done for the day. Go home and get started on the Bach. Better yet, go out and play for an extra half hour. Then go home and start on the Bach. And give it everything you've given this piece."

❧

IT STILL WASN'T entirely clear to me whether Mr. Kreitz had known Kabalevsky. He had once called him Comrade, but I wasn't really sure what that meant. Maybe this was a way to find out. Every time I saw him, he was filled with questions. What was I doing in my time off? What did I think about? How did I feel? I always had the feeling that kids were not allowed to ask old people questions. Or maybe I just kept forgetting to ask.

I brought Mr. Kreitz his Friday pot roast. As always, it was my last delivery of the day so I didn't have to get back to the deli. He asked me how I was, if I'd heard any interesting music, if I'd learned anything new. Then he fell silent for a moment and looked closely at me.

"What is it, Michael? Are you all right?"

I looked at my feet. "Yeah, I'm fine."

"But…?"

"Well, nothing."

He leaned over into my field of vision. *"But…?"*

"No, nothing really. Only you asked to hear the Kabalevsky, so I've been practicing it."

I did not tell him that it was the only thing I had been doing.

His face lit up. "Wonderful! So what's the problem?"

My mind raced. What *was* the problem? "I guess I'm afraid of making mistakes." I wanted to grab the words and cram them back down my throat.

He thought about what I said for a moment and then started to laugh. Not a great, big guffaw, but his little body just shook. He was enjoying the moment. I hadn't seen him laugh before. Nothing more than a little chuckle now and then.

I usually hated it when people laughed at me. I hated it when adults thought I was cute or sweet or charming. I felt little. I felt like a baby. The more charming they found me, the more I hated them. I tried to remember that grownups liked making other people laugh.

"Mistakes?" The quiet laughter continued. "Musicians don't make mistakes? They play everything perfectly?"

"Well, they do when they're playing for other people."

He tried to control his amusement. "First, no they don't. I've heard lots of musicians make *lots* of mistakes. You're confusing performance with what you hear on recordings. Recordings are note perfect. They have to be. So they're not always the most exciting performances. And second, from now on, I hope you'll do me the honor of not thinking about me as *other people*. Can you do that?"

I nodded but didn't know if I really could manage that. It was one thing to make mistakes in front of Lily or my mother. But in front of him? I didn't really know very much about him, but I knew that he knew something.

I sat down at the piano and played a few of the harder chords slowly, thinking about what went before and what came after. The sofa squeaked behind me.

I took a deep breath and then launched into it, listening hard to the notes, watching my fingers. Listening to the timing. Listening to the loud and soft. I made a few small mistakes but knew that it was more important to keep to the timing. Finally, I reached the end of the first movement and took another deep breath.

"Very nice," came his voice from behind me. Not happy. Not interested.

"Very nice?" I looked at him.

He put a smile on his face but said nothing. I could only imagine that it was a polite smile.

"Mister Kreitz. Very nice, but what?"

He thought for a moment. "Well, there's nothing *wrong* with it."

"Mister Kreitz…"

He grabbed the bridge of his nose and squeezed real hard. "It's just… there's so much you could do with it. I mean, just *imagine* what you could do with it. You return to the original theme… and then you play it just the same as the *first* time. Why! When we talk and we need to repeat our words—you know, for emphasis—do we say it the same way? Of course not! We change it so people will listen. Here's your chance to do something *new* with the theme. Kabalevsky is giving you the theme again so you can play it two different ways, not just repeat it— *same-same*. What's the interest in that?"

I did not have an answer. Everything I thought of just sounded stupid.

He stood up and stared at the piano.

"You know, music is eminently patient. It will let us

play its tunes wrong—and wrong again—for as long as we like, or don't like. It will just lie there on the page, minding its own business, as if to say, *It makes no difference to me how much you screw this up. Screw it up all you like, in fact.* It will never teach us the best way, the *most beautiful* way, to play it. And, when we finally discover a wonderful way to play something, we might be lucky enough to hear it, and we might not. But the dots and lines and squiggles on the page will never say *well done.* Its reward comes from us. From hearing it. From recognizing it."

"Or not."

"Or not," he chuckled. "Very true. And, even after you hear the most wonderful interpretation of the piece, someone else will come along and show you, *No, this is an even more beautiful interpretation.* I like to call it The Surprise of... *Of Course.* This way of playing is perfectly logical once you've heard it. After that, you know it could not have been played any other way. Before or since."

He placed his right hand over his heart. For a moment I thought he was going to pledge allegiance to the flag. He then put the index finger of his left hand on the outside of his right wrist. His thumb was wrapped around his wrist. He was showing me his fingers on the neck of a violin.

"You know, Jascha Heifetz completely changed the way all violinists transition between notes. For three hundred years, people have been sliding their fingers up the neck from one note to the other." He slid his index finger up his arm a few inches toward his elbow and then back down again. "Then Heifetz comes along and changes everything." He slid the same finger up his arm and, at the last moment, dropped his middle finger into place. "And then everyone said *Of course! This is the only way to play it.*"

"Could you show me what that sounds like? On your violin."

If I could put words to his face, they would have been *Shit, why did I do that?*

"Maybe. Someday." He recovered. Still the regret on his face. "But you can also hear The Surprise of... *Of Course* in unexpected twists and turns in music composition. Take the turning point in the first movement of Mozart's Fortieth Symphony. Mozart almost seems to be saying, *You weren't expecting that one, were you?*"

I nodded slowly. Did he really mean *take for instance* or something more specific?

"Well, do you know it?"

I nodded again, I think even more slowly.

"Michael, do you know Mozart's Fortieth, yes or no?"

I did the most difficult thing a thirteen-year-old can do.

"I guess not."

He stared hard at me.

"I mean... I *probably* know it. You know, if you played..."

"First of all, don't lie to me." He threw his head back and closed his eyes. "The *lies* I have had to put up with in my life. I want to share with you some of the things I know. But I would like to think of you as my friend if

I'm going to do that. That means *no lies*. So, if you don't know it, just say so. Second? Learn your classics, all right?" He took a deep breath. "I tell you what. Play it one more time. The Kabalevsky. I might interrupt you—talk or something—but just keep playing."

I turned back to the piano and tried to punch the notes, to bang the keys with my fingertips.

"*No,*" he shouted. "Start again! Start louder!"

I didn't know whether to feel confused or afraid—or both. And afraid of what? Afraid maybe of who Mr. Kreitz really was?

"That's right. Now *even* angrier. No! NO! Kabalevsky is furious! Stop! Stop playing!" His voice was shaking. "Come over here to my kitchen table. Think of something that makes you angry. *Really* angry. Something you hate."

What did I hate? I hated when my mother told me to do my homework. I hated the Vietnam War. No. That's not what he meant. What I *really* hated was Mr. Kreitz saying, *very nice*.

"Now make a fist and pound it on the table. That's angry? *That's* what you call angry? *Pound* the damn table, Michael! This is angry music!" *(It is?)* "Let me hear the anger! What makes you furious? So? *Show me!* Show me how angry you are. Let the music be the table. Let the table be the piano. Let the piano *be* the music. Feel it and then show it! Now back to the piano. *Bang the damn table and then bang the damn piano.*"

No one had ever talked to me this way. No one had ever talked to me *about music* this way. That was the difference. He wasn't treating me like a baby.

"First of all, stop playing all the right notes. Stop being so neat and tidy. You can't be furious and tidy." I looked up at him. A vein was exposed in his forehead. "*Show* me how furious he is. Furious that you must be a Soviet whore. A stooge. Furious at your medals that you get for making pretty music. Furious at your denunciations. For being branded a Formalist. And for groveling and simpering and apologizing just so you can fall back into the good favor of the Party. Even after they have disgraced you. *Ridiculed* you!"

He was perspiring. His hands were shaking.

"Mister Kreitz, did I do something wrong?"

At once, he must have realized what he looked like. He took a breath and closed his eyes. "No, of course not." He went over to his couch, his safe place, and sat down. He thought for a long moment. "Michael, I believe it is our duty to show people what beautiful music sounds like."

"Our duty?"

"Well, yes. You know, people like Kabalevsky and Khachaturian and so many others have not had the freedom to do that. Just to make a living, they have had to write music that *everyone* likes. Can you even imagine that? How absolutely boring. And how sad that Kabalevsky is best known for his *Comedian's Galop* and Khachaturian for his *Sabre Dance*. These pieces of… *of crap* belong in the circus—*literally!* Anything more complicated than music to accompany spinning plates on Ed Sullivan and they'll be denounced for writing bourgeois music that people actually have to *think about.* I mean, *perish the thought!*"

"But, Mister Kreitz. *Our* duty?"

"Yes, Michael. *Our* duty." He focused on me. "What's the matter? Haven't you got it in you? Why do want to play music? To be famous and that's it?"

I felt my face get warm. "Well, not that."

"No? You don't want all the fame—the money and the admiration? And the women?"

Actually that didn't sound so bad, but I could hear the derision. Maybe even disgust. What could be so terrible about it?

"Michael, have you ever even thought about why you want to make music—*need* to make music?"

How would he know that?

"Of course you haven't. Not at your age."

Now he was talking down to me. I *really* didn't like that.

"Mister Kreitz, do I have to think about why I do everything, just like you? Can't I just like making music?" This might be dangerous territory but I couldn't stop now. "I mean, I don't just sit around in my room thinking *why this* and *why that*."

The room echoed with our voices for a moment.

"I apologize." He sighed. "Of course, right now, you can enjoy making music and that can be enough. But I dare to predict that the moment will come when there will be more to it."

♪

I SPENT THE NEXT week wondering why I had spent so much time with him. What had I hoped to gain? What had I wanted to learn? Who needs to visit an old man just to get yelled at? Didn't I have enough musical input between my real music teacher, and my mother—who *was* a music teacher—and my practice? Did I really need more? Who was I helping? Why did I even give a shit?

Music, *my music,* was enough. I was learning plenty. I loved what I was learning. It was enough, and fast enough, for me.

And that's when it dawned on me. Of course, it would continue to dawn on me—whatever *it* is. Pretty notes weren't enough. And using an instrument to translate what's inside to the outside. I got it. That's why it's called an instrument.

I HAD TO SAVE UP six dollars. That was hard, but it allowed me to take the subway up to Sam Goody's in Midtown and buy an LP of Bach keyboard concertos. I needed to hear someone else play the new piece. I needed to know the right way.

It would take me months just to *look* at all these records in this temple—which you could mistake for a train-terminal—and years to listen to them. Rows upon rows of LPs and singles were illuminated by strips of bare fluorescent tubes overhead. Each corner had oversized speakers playing different music—Beethoven there, French *chansons* there, dissonant jazz there.... Here, too, time slowed. People floated, dreamlike, from one aisle to the next. They stood riffling through stacks of records. The people in the aisles seemed to keep changing but the search continued. Were they looking for something specific or did the pleasure come simply from surrounding oneself with all this music?

Over the course of years, this place would welcome me into its fold. I would be one of the thousands who sought solace in this expanse. The chaos of people and music would not be forbidding but joyous and comforting. Right now, it was just big.

I headed straight for the signs that directed me to

BAROQUE and then BACH and finally BACH KEYBOARD and started my search. I was dizzied by the quantity, but I expected to find what I needed if I just kept searching.

"Studying something new?"

He could have just as easily shouted, *"BOO!"* The world around me had fallen away. And New Yorkers didn't talk to each other. I whirled around to see an old man—at least forty—with a badge hanging from his shirt pocket. It read, *HI! MY NAME IS* **RALPH**. I wondered why he had to wear that. I wasn't ever going to yell, "Hey, Ralph" across the store. I was pretty sure no one else would, either.

"Uh… yeah, actually I am."

"Maybe I can help."

"Oh… well… that'd be great. Thanks." I patted my pockets in search of the paper with all the information.

"All I really need is the BWV number."

I stared at him.

"Well, I'm assuming it's Bach if you're over here"

He saw my face and started to giggle.

"Hey, it's my job. This is what I do all day." I tried to imagine what it would be like, surrounded by all these records, every day. I stared at all the stacks and stared back at him. He smiled again. "It's a living."

I found the paper. "It's BWV one thousand and fifty-six."

"Ten-fifty-six. OK, that's over here. You can choose between piano solo, harpsichord solo, or orchestral arrangement with either instrument."

There must have been twenty different recordings. I started to look at the pictures on the album covers, the performers' names, the prices.

"Can I make it easy for you?"

I looked at him blankly.

"There's really only one worth having." He pulled up an album of a man with a bony face and greasy hair sitting too low at the keyboard. "Don't be put off by his looks. This guy whips 'em all."

THE MAN AT Sam Goody's was right. The funny-looking guy in the too-low chair took sheet music and turned it into something untouchable. I was being ambushed by a realization. This was what all good musicians were doing—turning ink on paper into magic.

I don't know how many times I played the record. First, I listened. Then I listened and memorized. Then I put the record on, ran over to the piano, and tried to play along. That didn't work because I had to keep stopping. I had to keep playing each passage to get the touch just right. The speed of each note. The weight. The space between the notes. Sometimes he came down right on top of the beat, sometimes he was just behind. But it was always intentional—always—though I didn't know how I could tell.

So, the notes weren't the problem—not the notes themselves. It was the spaces in between the notes that were hard. The length of each note. The pressure on the keys. The attack. I might have to do the unthinkable.

Yes, I would have to do the unthinkable.

"Well, I was wondering when—*or if*—you were ever going to come to me."

My mother was washing the dinner dishes. I didn't

have to wash the dishes if I promised to practice for an hour. It wasn't entirely fair as she could clear up in fifteen minutes but those were the rules. "Of course I can help. I'm glad to help. *I'm a music teacher ferchrissake!*"

I knew that. I just didn't want her to be my music teacher.

She dried her hands, dipped a finger into a jar of cold cream next to the sink, and rubbed it into her hands.

"Follow me. I'm gonna play you two different versions of the same piece. I don't have the Bach, but I'll play you something that I think shows what I mean."

She led the way to the corner where the hi-fi slumbered, riffled through our record collection— nowhere near my father's record—and pulled out two LPs. One bore the label *Beethoven Klaviersonaten – Volume 1*. It had a photo of a man seated next to a piano, one elbow up on the piano's beam, smiling up into the camera. The other read *The World's Most Beautiful Piano Music*. It featured a Technicolor photo of a piano with a vase of roses in front of the lid prop. She put that one on first.

"This is a piano sonata called the *Pathétique*. Tell me what you think."

After about two minutes, she turned the volume to zero and lifted the tone arm.

"So?"

"Sounds hard."

She thought about that for a minute. "I think that depends on what you call hard."

"Hard. You know? Hard? Like, the notes are hard to play?"

"Well, *I* don't think they're hard to play. Millions of people play this piece. Oh, God, I've hurt your feelings." She screwed up her face and rubbed her palms against her forehead—never a good sign. "Listen, I'm not saying you're good or you're bad, or *anything*." She slowed to enunciate every word. "Believe it or not, I'm only asking you what you think of the piece."

I wanted to argue with her. *Of course* she was commenting on me. She always did.

"Can we please just stay on the subject? I think I can help you here. I'm just trying to make a point. It's about how important performance is. It's not about the notes. It's the performance that's hard—harder than the notes. Sure, OK, maybe the notes *are* hard, but lots of people can play them. The point is, not very many people can play them *beautifully*. That's why I'm playing these two recordings. That's all I'm trying to say here. OK? Can you believe me?"

I wanted to walk out.

"Yeah, OK."

"Michael, please. Bear with me for a few minutes. Just tell me what you heard in the piece."

I shrugged.

"Is it interesting? Is it emotional? Is it boring?"

"Well, it's not boring. There's a lot going on. There's lots of different stuff going on."

"Different themes?"

"Well, yeah, but it starts out very heavy and gets faster."

She nodded and gave her teacher smile. "There are three different themes just in this one movement. It changes keys a few times. It goes from minor to major to minor and back again."

"That's crazy. It does all that but it doesn't sound, you know, messy."

"Beethoven was a pretty smart guy that way."

"How do you do that? How do you write music that people want to listen to three hundred years later?"

"Well, more like a hundred-sixty, but even so."

She was already on her way over to the hi-fi again. She put on the second record and turned up the volume. It was the same piece, obviously, but it could have hardly been more different. The louds were louder. The pianist took a longer pause after the first chord. Some of the pauses were hardly pauses at all, but they were there. How long is a pause, anyway? The long runs in the right hand were so clear and clean. How do you play so fast and yet make each note its own?

"It's like each note is… well, not exactly staccato, but separate."

She smiled and nodded.

"How do you do that?"

"OK, I think I understand your question. It's not about practice—well, or it's not *only* about practice. It's about talent. It about knowing where to do what. It's about knowing what to practice. It's the difference between good and great."

The music was still playing. We stopped talking to listen some more. It made me want to play. It made me want to run away. People could write and paint and make sounds that went far beyond words like *art* and *beauty* and *creativity*, and these words had no meaning. Human beings were capable of expressing beauty that outpaced their ability to describe it. This pianist could not even know that he had done something to change me.

"It's… I don't know what to call it. I love it."

She smiled. "Me too."

"How do you learn how to do this? Can anyone learn how to do this?"

"Are you asking me if you can learn how to do this?"

Now that she mentioned it…

She shrugged. "Not everyone can learn how to play like this and I don't know why. It comes down to talent and I don't know what talent is. I don't think anyone knows."

I watched her face. She looked lost.

"Mom?"

She shook herself awake.

"Listen, there's no substitute for practice, but there's no substitute for talent." Her eyes sidled to me. "And before you get the wrong idea, there's no substitute for talent, but there's also no substitute for practice."

❧

I WENT TO THE piano and opened Bach BWV 1056, II: *Air*.

Practice became the only thing that interested me. Reiteration and repetition and rehashing and rephrasing. Days of experimentation passed before I even got to the end. I would practice until I got bored and then I'd just practice the hardest parts. I didn't have to think about whether they sounded good or bad. I just had to get the notes right. I could worry about how pretty they sounded later, but first I had to make them *sound*. I played the same passage again and again and again and again and again and again and again and again and again and again—sometimes just three notes in a difficult transition, sometimes four, sometimes more. If no one was around, I brought the TV over next to the piano, put it on a chair where I could see it, turn on a baseball game or cartoons, and play the notes. I didn't have to listen to what I was playing. I just had to teach my fingers to move in the right direction.

But then there was that next step—making it beautiful. How do you know when music sounds good? How could I know when the music I made sounded good? Would I even know?

𝄾

WHAT HAPPENS WHEN we gain awareness? What changes in that moment when we understand something we did not get a moment before? Is it all a question of a couple of neurons firing in the brain that had failed to fire until now? If all these circuits are talking to each other at some incomprehensible speed, why does awareness creep up on us so slowly? Of course, we have the odd *aha* moment, but—at least for me—those flashes of light are far outnumbered by the molasseslike fade-ups from ignorance to cognizance. *Is* it down to nothing more than a change in brain chemistry? *Something* must be changing in our minds, of course. Johan Sebastian Bach was born in 1685 and died in 1750. That is a fact. We learn it. We remember it, or do our best to remember it. And, when I am able to recall it, something in my brain says *Thanks for the memory.*

But what about when it's more than just facts? What happened when, for the first moment in my life, I understood what Bach had been trying to tell me two hundred fifty years earlier? *This* was awareness. Or is that too strong? I was thirteen. Who knows how much I understood of anything? I doubt I fully understood the lyrics to "The Times They Are a-Changin'" for that matter. But something changed. My brain wasn't thanking me for facts—my whole *body* was thanking me. But for what? How could it be that I understood something now that I had heard before yet had not understood? There was something so incredibly *smart* about Bach's music and, now, I could hear it.

If I played the music very slowly—*very* slowly—the notes clashed and fought. They banged against each other. When I played it at normal speed, it had the click of a key in a lock. It fell perfectly into place. I understood. Bach was writing it that way on purpose. We can just barely register the dissonances as they fly by but, before we even have the time to let them in, the door has unlocked and we get that little tickle. Somewhere inside, my body says *of course* each time it registers something I thought did not even belong there a moment before—even before I have time to *say* it doesn't belong. So, it is a surprise. And then it is *of course*.

I sat quietly at the piano trying to figure out where, if not in my brain, this change was taking place. Was it in my spine? My stomach? My balls? I had heard people say that a particular performance had touched their hearts. What did that mean? Rock songs were always using the word *heart* for something—something like love. Someone's heart was always yearning or breaking or tumbling. But this had nothing to do with love.

The next logical question—perhaps even a life-changing question—arose. If I could hear the beauty in music, could I make it, too?

𝄡

WHAT WAS THE opposite of dread? I don't just mean happy anticipation. Because dread was all I had ever felt going to Lily which, when I thought about it, was odd. Her home had always been a safe haven for me—the closest thing to a place where I could do no wrong. And still, I always felt I was letting her down—until now, I hoped.

We had made a deal that I would play the solo part on one piano and she would play the orchestral part on the other. When she was satisfied with my work, we would switch parts.

"So!" She examined my face. "Are you ready? Would you like to play it for me one time before I go to the other piano?"

I smiled. "I'm ready." I wondered if I had ever told her the truth before now.

Her half-smile said *If you say so.* She walked to the second piano and sat down. I opened the canvas bag my mother had given me to carry my sheet music (with *DON'T BUY JUDY BOND BLOUSES* emblazoned on it), took out the music, and placed it on the lectern. I sat at my piano and looked over at her. She raised one hand to where I could see it and counted to three as a conductor does.

"Lily, that's too slow."

She looked a little surprised.

"Sorry, can we do it just a little faster?"

"Well, then, you give me the tempo."

There was only one tempo. I had locked it in. Play anything else for me, crowd my head with any other noise. Then ask me for the tempo to BWV 1056 *Largo* and I can give it to you.

We started in and the voices interlocked—an acoustic enactment of the two pianos nestled into each other's shape. I'd had an idea of what to expect because I had listened to the record so many times. I had experienced something similar when I played guitar songs with my friends. I always enjoyed it when we were able conspire to make something special of the latest Beatles song. Still, being part of this particular conversation was different. This was all about balance. It was about listening and responding, about mirroring each other's expression. And Bach... Bach understood something about interlocking voices.

The *Largo* is such a delicate piece—a minimalist work of glass sculpture. There is not an extraneous note. Nothing goes to waste. Play it right and you have an exquisite construction of pitch and weight and color and juxtaposition. Fail to match the voices and it becomes a heavy-handed clunk of sounds, worse than the simplest children's piece banged out on a toy piano. A piece of plastic schlock in a store window. So far, we were doing pretty well. *Pretty* well.

I stopped.

She looked up. "Lose your place?"

"No, that's not it." I didn't know how this was going to sound. "You're not... Can you play it a little different?"

"I'm what? I'm not playing it right?" It took her a moment to take that in.

Who the hell did I think I was? The look on Lily's face told me she was thinking the same thing.

"OK, what's the right way, then?" Her voice wasn't entirely cheerful.

"I'm sorry. There has to be another way to play it."

She shrugged. "There are *a thousand* other ways to play it, but you'd better be ready to explain yourself."

What was the right word? "Can you make it, well… crisper?"

"*Crisper?* So, not *crispissimo?*" She was not smiling.

I felt myself blush. "I'm sorry, Lily. Just play it your way."

She thought for a moment. "You know what? I'm not gonna do that. You have an idea? I want to hear about it. You realize these aren't just piano lessons. They're music lessons. You're learning about music. Well, now I want to know what you've learned. I want to hear what you're hearing."

What had I gotten myself into?

She sighed. "You know, I thought about getting all pissed off at you there—you, who have taken your own damn time finding the music. But you have, now."

I had?

"So I want to know about it. Just tell me what you're hearing. Crisper? Tell me what you mean."

There was no getting out of this.

"Well, you're coming down too hard."

"I am?" Her face had not softened. She looked down at her keyboard and then back at me. "Define *coming down*, please."

"Well, it's not so much that you're too loud, but

you're holding the notes too long."

Now she looked confused. "But I like it that way." Was she trying to confuse me or was I just stupid? "Damn it, Michael. If you're going to correct your teacher, you'd better be ready to explain yourself. You don't like the way I'm playing it? Tell me why not."

I could feel my brain scurrying in five directions at once. "It… it makes everything muddy."

"Muddy? You want me to play it all staccato?" She jabbed at the notes, harder than was necessary. It sounded ridiculous and she knew it. She was taunting me.

"*C'mon,* Lily. You know I don't mean that."

"You know what? I really don't. I have a vague idea, but I *really* want you to tell me."

I had to think hard. "Actually the staccato is closer to what I'm hearing." This was useless. I didn't know how to say what I wanted. "I'm sorry. Just play it the way you—"

"Sorry, Michael, I'm not gonna do that. I'm not gonna let you walk away from this. *Tell me what you mean, for godsakes.*"

I wanted to play her part for her but I didn't know it. I realized that, if I was going to talk about the music, I had to know it—all of it. I pressed my hands over my eyes and listened to something inside.

"Is there a way of playing that's just a little bit less than staccato? There must be a name for that."

She listened to the air for a moment and thought. "Well, how about *portato*?" She played it again. It was better but still wrong.

Only one thing was clear—she was insisting that I

grow up.

"That's better… I guess. Now, can you leave just the tiniest space in between?" Was this right? I still hadn't answered the *who-do-I-think-I-am* part.

She stared at her keyboard and thought. "So… a slurred staccato."

She demonstrated it. I smiled and nodded.

"Yeah?"

She counted off.

The room became cool and dark and, again, I could hear crickets singing. Then something else happened. I believe it was the first time I ever stopped thinking. The walls and the piano stool under me fell away and I was weightless. I was only vaguely aware of my fingers, but mostly that I was guiding them with my eyes. My breath was not there to take in air but to push my hands. And there was no difference between my hands and the piano keys and the notes that flowed out.

We finished and were quiet for a moment. I was perspiring lightly.

I awoke.

"What's so funny?" I watched Lily's face closely.

"I dunno. I just never thought I'd see the day."

𝄢

OVER THE WEEK that followed, I thought about a song I could play for Mr. Kreitz when I next saw him. There was no point in playing a four-square, four-chord song. It would have to be sophisticated. "Wooly Bully" and " 'Enery the Eighth" were fun and easy, but complex times called for, well, complex measures.

I finally came up with The Beatles' "I'll Be Back." It is melodic and emotional. It's also hard to play. It switches back and forth between major and minor keys—between hope and despair. Not the kind of subtlety you hear, or even think of, in pop music. Most important, it would show that my music was not all *Papa-Oom-Mow-Mow* and *Yeah-Yeah-Yeah*.

It's a typical John Lennon song in that John liked to mess with time. It has three sections, not counting the exposition, so it is immediately asymmetrical. That might not be enough to wrong-foot the listener, yet each section is twelve measures long instead of the standard eight or sixteen. And, then for no reason—or for every reason—he changes the sixth measure of the B section to six-quarter time and makes the C section *nine* measures long—again with a final measure of six-four at the end.

To add to the tension, he starts with a two-measure exposition instead of the standard four-measure start in common time.

Even the song's key is uncertain. There are arguments for transcribing it in A Major or A Minor. The exposition is in A Major, but the first section starts in A Minor and ends in A Major. The B section starts in F-sharp Minor—the relative minor—and the C section starts in B Minor. That resolves in E, which carries us back to the A section which, again, ends in a major chord. If we like to think that songs in major keys are happy and minor keys are sad, this song puts that myth to rest. If the A Major resolution is a smile at all, it is a sad one. If anything, it is a shrug of resignation. Finally, everything is played on acoustic guitars. There is no percussion or electric sound to offer any inner strength.

George Harrison had the idea to add an F-sharp, B, and E in a rising line—part of the A pentatonic scale, and which do nothing to suggest either major or minor key— before each A section. It contributes even further to the tenuousness of the structure. It puts everything even more out of balance. The line could all fall apart at any moment, but it does not.

Then, just to keep it interesting, John plays triplets over the steady four-four strum—only in the third measure of each A section. It was a trick he had used in "All My Loving" and it works well here. The structure is:

EXPOSITION

A^1-A^2 - B - A^1-A^2 –

C

A^1-A^2 - B - A^1-A^2 - A^1

FADEOUT

The fadeout alternates major and minor chords in standard four-quarter time, so it mirrors the A sections. But other than the protracted fadeout at the end, the structure forms a perfect, symmetrical palindrome.

And it all sounds so logical. The Surprise of… *Of course!*

But all these components, contributing factors, musical variations, adornments, embellishments—the major-minor, the triplets, the symmetry and asymmetry—do much more than create interest. They create terrible uncertainty. They form the perfect musical reflection of the lyric.

The words describe nothing but loose ends. Unfinished business. The singer admits his complete vulnerability. And the music confesses, as strongly as the words, *I am defenseless.*

This was going to be hard. Maybe I could leave the second guitar's triplets out of my piano part. That was going too far. Then maybe I could leave out the C section—excise the C section. Then I realized it was impossible to play and sing at the same time.

Maybe "Yesterday" would be easier.

Yeah, he'd like that better.

℥

FRIDAY CAME AROUND and I could think of little other than bringing Mr. Kreitz his pot roast. Finally, when Mr. Kahanah asked me if I was willing to bring it over, I had to put effort into looking as nonchalant as I possibly could. To be emotional about this was not allowed. I could not show that I cared. Not at thirteen.

So it was with just the slightest bit of disappointment that Mr. Kreitz did not ask me to play music at all. He just seemed to want to talk. I was sure he would have been glad to listen had I volunteered, but I decided to save it for another moment.

"I just have one question for you. Do you have a moment for one question?"

I did my fast shrug to say *I guess so*.

"Since my retirement I've had plenty of time to think and not very many friends with whom to discuss my ideas."

OK, so maybe he did have *some* friends, but it did not occur to me to ask him, *retirement from what?*

"I've been thinking about our conversation of last week."

So had I.

He sat down on his couch and scratched his chin. He looked at his piano—or not so much at it as through it.

"I got the distinct feeling that you are a music lover. Would I be right?"

I suddenly regretted keeping secret—or at least not saying out loud—that I loved music. Why should it be so important to hide the idea, the feeling, *the fact* that I loved music? So? I loved music. What could be so terrible about that? At age thirteen, there was clearly something dangerous about revealing personal information to strangers. It's mine, it's not yours. Who knows *what* you'll go and do with my things? I'm giving you my keys—to something, anyway. I'm just not sure what. Now, though, it was clear that I had failed at keeping it a secret. Or had I succeeded in letting him know?

"I like it a lot." I still couldn't quite bear to use the word *love*. What was so dangerous about that word?

He was unfazed by my reluctance. In fact, he didn't even seem to notice.

"Even if we love different kinds of music, we still share this love, do we not?"

I nodded.

"So here is my question. *Why* do we love music?"

I looked at him in stupid amazement. I was used to people asking me things, but they were the questions young people are so used to hearing—even from the intellectuals around my mother's brunch table. What grade was I in. Did I like to read. Did I prefer The Beatles or The Stones. This man was asking me a *why* question. Did he actually take me seriously or did he just have no one else to talk to? Did he really want an answer or was he just thinking aloud? I think the stupid look persisted.

Was this a test? I saw a book title, *On Music*, on his shelf. Did that hold the answer? I had been waiting all my short life for this moment—for someone to ask me an adult question. And now it came as a surprise.

"I… uh…"

"Think of it this way." He looked around the room. I wasn't sure if he was looking for something in particular. "I've been giving this some thought, you see. Have you learned anything about evolution at school?"

"Well, sure. I guess a little, anyway."

He stood up slowly. The late afternoon sun had made its way to his front window and, without even thinking about it, he moved into the light.

"So, for instance, I guess you've learned that we've evolved to run and climb and, well, even *to think*, so we could hunt for food and make tools."

I nodded and wondered vaguely where he was taking this.

"We also evolved to be able to form societies." He glanced at me. "You know, form groups larger than our own families—like tribes or clans."

In fact, we had not learned about that. It was a brand-new idea to me.

"And, as our brains evolved and developed, we learned better how to interpret sounds. First we learned how to distinguish safe sounds from dangerous ones. You know, 'Is that the sound of a lion or a pussycat?' or even, 'Is that a wild dog or a tame dog?'"

I nodded to keep him talking.

"And over many years—I mean over five or ten or fifteen thousand years—we learned to *make* sounds that other people understood. We learned to make *words*. But now here's my question. When did we learn to make sounds that other people understood, but that weren't words? When did we learn to make *music*? Was that before we learned to talk or after?"

What a strange thought.

"I don't know."

"No, nor do I." He smiled sadly at me. "What I don't understand is, how our brains—which are designed to distinguish dangerous sounds from safe ones, and even words—should also know how to make music."

I had been waiting all this time to have an adult conversation. I just hadn't expected it to be this conversation.

"After all, if we know the sound of danger, then we live longer. We survive. We pass that ability on to our children. The people who don't recognize the dangerous sounds—well, they don't survive. And, people who can make sounds that other people understand also have a better chance of surviving and passing that ability on. But how do we move from *this* to the ability—or even the desire—to make music? And, what's more, why we should feel *emotions* when we hear music?"

I nodded again. I had no idea what to say.

"How is it that we have the ability to decide that this person makes sounds on this machine that evoke stronger emotions than that person? I mean, what are we? We're apes! We—*people*—have spent most of our history living in small clutches in the plains of Africa and Asia. Our brains are evolved to help us eat. To protect ourselves. To be fruitful and multiply. To defend our young. So why should we respond emotionally to music? You know, I gave up on God a long time ago. But, who else *but* God would provide us with the ability to love beauty? To want *to create* beauty! To want to make others appreciate the beauty we create! *Is* this a plea for the existence of God? And, if so, why should it be in God's interest for us to respond emotionally to groups of pitch, rhythm, and dynamics?"

I felt a little dizzy.

"And then, who was the first person to play a violin? And the day *before* that, what had that person been playing? What was *that* instrument called? What did it look like? And the instrument before *that*? And, how did he know how to play it? Who could have possibly had the idea to stretch a length of twisted animal intestines tight and thin over a wooden box and then pull a bunch of horsehair across it? I mean, that's all a violin is."

It was?

"You know, Shakespeare asked the same question. *'Isn't it strange that sheep guts should pull our souls out of our bodies?'* Something like that. So he was wondering the same thing—and he probably wasn't the first to ask that question, either."

He clasped his hands and started walking slowly across the room. Nowhere in particular. Just to walk.

"And here's another one. When did we come to realize that a student could learn from his teacher and then *surpass* him? Become better than his teacher! How is that possible? How do you learn from someone else— everything they know—and, ultimately, learn *more* than they are able to teach you?"

He turned on his heel and walked back to the window.

"When was the very first time—I mean *the very first time*—someone made music that caused someone else to respond emotionally? To have a deep emotional response? Isn't that a strange idea? That we should hear music and feel emotional about it? When was the first time that someone *cried* upon hearing a piece of music? Is that what the player, or composer, was trying to do at that moment? Or had it been purely by chance? A happy accident. How does that work? I can only imagine that it started with singing. We had our voices before we had instruments. Don't you think? Or do you think it started with people banging on logs?"

Finally, here was a chance to add something to the conversation. I could *make* it a conversation. I knew something.

"Well, we learned at school about how Australian aborigines could sing maps across the wilderness."

He squinted at me. Did he not understand or was I just standing in the dark? Or had he forgotten that I was there?

"Yeah, they have songs that say things like, *This path goes to that water hole, and then to the next water hole, and all the way to the ocean.*"

He raised his eyebrows. I had managed to surprise him.

"But you mean the lyrics, yes? Not the notes of the song, I assume."

"Uh, no. I guess the lyrics." I shrugged. "I *guess* so."

"Fascinating to be sure. But this must be a later development. *Music* is not language. It can *use* language, but it's not language itself. It's nonsense! Yet it makes us feel all kinds of things. It can make us cry!"

"Well, I always hear about people calling music the international language."

He thought about this for a moment. "Yes, I've heard that, too. But is it? Is it really a language? After all, it doesn't have nouns and verbs. I mean, I can't say *I went to the grocery store* in Violin, or *Pass the salt* in Brahms."

I STARTED THINKING about the best way to just drop by Mr. Kreitz's house, and how long I should wait until I did.

A few days later I awoke to deep-throated, distant thunder. The skies played the opening chords to "Downtown." The summer air felt warm and heavy on my body. A light breeze fragrant with green, thick on the lungs, meandered through my window. The sky was darkening—a warning of things to come. Here, on the ground floor, there was hardly any wind. Yet the treetops stirred restlessly, turning their heads, looking for the coming storm. Sparrows collected over the street screeing with enthusiasm at the expected meal of thunder flies.

Then came the sound of rain falling through summer air, chattering against the leaves. It made our quiet side street in the middle of the city smell like a forest. Music could not capture this sound. Composers had certainly tried, but it always sounded fake.

I raised myself up on my elbows to look out the window. This was perfect. There would be no punchball today.

At around noon, I picked up two sandwiches from the deli. I came equipped with answers because Mr. and Mrs.

Kahanah always had questions. No, the sandwiches were for me and a friend. No, not a girlfriend, just a friend. I tried to pay for the food as it wasn't a workday for me. Finally, after much good-natured argument, they agreed to let me pay the cost price which, Mr. Kahanah said, came to thirty-five cents. He pocketed the money rather than putting it in the cash register.

I was taking a chance. I couldn't be sure the Hermit would be home, but I was guessing that he got out even less than he was willing to let on. I lifted the knocker and tapped it four times as I had always done. I hoped it would tip him off to my presence.

There was a long wait, but then there always was. Finally the deadbolt snapped back. The door opened and his expressionless face appeared, as expressionless as ever, around the doorjamb. He then broke into a bright smile.

"Michael! But… I didn't order anything today." There was confusion behind his eyes.

"No, I know. I was just taking you up on your invitation." He was silent. Had he forgotten? Maybe he hadn't meant it. "You said if I ever felt like coming around and talking about music…"

He gasped. Not a theatrical gasp like my mother sometimes did. Genuine, I think.

"Well, I'm honored!"

How could he possibly be honored by my desire to talk about music? He knew a thousand times more than I did. But I could see by his expression that he wasn't joking.

I followed him inside.

"I hope you like it. It's my favorite—pastrami and chopped liver on rye with mustard."

He giggled in a way that allowed me to imagine him as a younger person. "Wow, that's quite a combination, but it sounds good. Why don't you bring it into the kitchen? We can make a proper mess in there."

I had never been past his living room. Everything there was neat and tidy. With the exception of the hi-fi set, it looked as if it hadn't been remodeled since the nineteen-forties. In one corner there was a tiny square table with two chairs, one of which looked well worn and one which looked practically untouched.

"I'm afraid I only have coffee, tea, and water to drink."

Damn, I should have thought to bring sodas.

"Water's fine, thanks." I hated water.

"You sure? Well, I think I'll make myself a cup of tea. You don't want some?"

"Uhm, OK." I didn't particularly like tea. The way my mother made it, it always tasted bitter. "Just not too strong."

He nodded, weighed the kettle in his hand, and turned on the flame under it.

"No-no. Not strong. I like it quite sweet with a squeeze of lemon."

"Actually that's how my grandfather drinks his tea, with a lump of sugar between his teeth—except really strong. Too strong for me. He says it's not tea if you can't stand your spoon in it."

"Ah, so your grandparents are Russian!"

I suppose I shouldn't have been surprised. "Well, yeah. Except that they were pretty young when they came here."

He chuckled. "Anyway, that was how we drank tea back there. Now I just stir it in. Not very good for your teeth. Or, should I say, *very* good if you like holes in your teeth."

"So… you weren't born in America."

Something like amusement came across his face. "No, I most certainly was not born in America. But I escaped the Soviet Union when I was pretty young. I was in my early twenties."

"You escaped?"

He was busy opening the paper sandwich wrappings. Getting napkins. Cutting lemon wedges. Rinsing off the cutting board and washing the knife. Pouring hot water into the teapot. Plopping teabags up and down. Setting out the sugar bowl. He was busy with everything except answering my question.

"Mister Kreitz, you escaped?"

He breathed in as if to say something, but did not. He only let out a sigh. He breathed in again and, again, he waited. His head was tilting from one side to the other. I felt bad for asking but, now, the question was out there.

He poured out two cups and brought them to the table. I put two big scoops of sugar in mine and stirred for a long time. It gave me something to do while I waited.

"Do you know who Sergei Rachmaninoff was? Do you know anything about Mstislav Rostropovich? Or Dmitri Shostakovich? Or your friend Dmitry Kabalevsky?" He pronounced the names in a way that I could not have possibly managed. It was when he said the names that I could hear the old country.

"Well, sure. I mean, a little." I hoped he couldn't see I was bending the truth. They were little more than names that I'd heard my mother use in passing. She probably played some of their chamber music with her quartet.

He smiled. "Even so, I'm willing to bet you don't know what they went through just in order to make music."

"I guess not." Clearly there was no point in lying. Still, I found it hard to expose my ignorance.

He bit into his sandwich, really filled his mouth, and then chewed and chewed. He stirred sugar into his tea. Squeezed in lemon. Stirred some more. It was time to eat, I guessed, so I took a bite of my sandwich. There was nothing to do but wait.

Finally, he put down his sandwich, sat back, and thought.

"Some left. Some stayed. Most who stayed became conformists. They played the game, just so they could make music and care for their families. That's not too much to ask, is it? I mean, if you *have* to make music—if all you can do is make music—then you do what is asked of you. That's normal isn't it? Even so, some people left. Some left the easy way—by walking into an American embassy in a European city. Or hopping on a steamer. Easy. That meant leaving your parents and families and friends behind. Never seeing them again. Never hearing another word. That's the easy way." He looked at me, or more like sized me up. "I was twenty-four years old."

I tried to imagine what that meant. I was thirteen. My

brother was nineteen. I tried to build pictures in my head but had nothing to work with.

"Then there's the hard way. Just after the Revolution, Sergei Rachmaninoff put his wife and children in a horse-drawn sled and took them from Petrograd to Helsinki with nothing more than some sheet music in his pocket. Two hundred and fifty miles across the snowfields in the winter of nineteen-seventeen. I don't mind telling you the winter of nineteen-seventeen was more than a little cold. And then from there to Stockholm and *from there* to Copenhagen. That's leaving the hard way. But, he was descended from nobility, so his next stop was the labor camp, even if he did or said nothing. So I suppose he had no other choice."

He took a sip of tea and thought again.

To me, all of this sounded like some fairytale. None of this could be real. People don't act this way. People don't treat others this way. I didn't know what it would take—in me—to believe him.

"But some of them did something *even more* difficult. Some people stayed... and then fought the system. Those are the really brave ones. I mean, *really* brave. Mstislav Rostropovich has never stopped dissenting, but the Soviet government is powerless to stop him simply because he is a magnificent musician. Only recently they gave him the Lenin Prize for being a Working Class Hero. What else could they do? This way it looks like he's been making all that wonderful music especially for the Fatherland. 'You see? He's the perfect Soviet Citizen!' They hate him—and he hates them—but they can't stop him and he refuses to stop. This takes a kind of bravery that I cannot even imagine."

We were silent. I took a sip of tea and I could see my grandparents sipping tea in Russia.

Again, I tried to create some kind of picture. "You never saw your family again?"

He pressed his lips together. Tilted his head to one side. "I put word through, from friend to friend to friend, to tell them I was safe. I couldn't write letters because they would only be intercepted, and possibly even put them in more danger than I had already done, just by leaving. They would be made culpable for my counter-revolutionary thinking. After all, if I was counter-revolutionary, then they certainly must be."

I made a mental note to look up *counter-revolutionary* when I got home.

"And you didn't hear anything from them."

"No. Nothing." He gave a sad smile. "As a young man I thought, maybe if I played loud enough and well enough, my family back home could hear me. It would be a way of calling to them—*I'm all right. I'm safe.*"

I watched him closely but he was impassive. I could only guess that he had gotten used to the idea after all this time. Or maybe he just couldn't bear to think about it. The only thing I noticed was, the longer we talked, the stronger his Russian accent got.

"Instead, America made me a hero… for running away from my homeland. *That* I find just about as hypocritical as the Soviets and their awards. If anything, they should be applauding Rostropovich for standing up to the Soviet system—not someone who imperils his family by running to the so-called Free World."

"You got medals?"

He chuckled. "As a matter of fact I did. Well, one medal. But that's not what I mean. Everyone wanted to see this bright young thing who had chosen to reject the Soviet Union and make the United States his home. The way they paraded me around, I felt like some Olympic athlete who had decided to play for the winning team. I'll never really know if I was truly a good fiddle player or just a way for America to gloat at the enemy."

"You don't think you're—you were—a good violinist?"

Again that tilt of the head. "It's a fair question. For me, the question is, would I have gotten all that attention if I were a violinist growing up in New Jersey. That's what I'll never know."

As I cycled home, I remembered a moment from the first time we had met. He had said something like, *You don't go hungry living here in Greenwich Village.* Something like that.

}

IT IS HARD TO DESCRIBE, or imagine, what Russia looked like in 1918. The country was wrestling its way out of the First World War having won nothing and lost anywhere up to five million soldiers and civilians. Officials from the fledgling Soviet Union signed the Treaty of Brest-Litovsk to stop attacks from the Central Powers by ceding the Baltic States, Poland, and Ukraine. The treaty may have lasted all of nine months—from March to November of 1918—but it was enough to remove the country from the conflict. Russia's involvement in the war had been the Tsar's idea and he was out of the picture, under house arrest. The Bolshevik government needed its strength elsewhere.

In the same way that you can pull so hard on a door that you find yourself falling backward, so did the country fall straight into civil war. True, that war was already underway. But, with Germany and the Ottoman Empire out of the way, it could fall entirely into a battle that was to its own interest—or get mired in it.

In fact, as early as October of 1914, Vladimir Lenin had decried the Great War as "...imperialist, predatory, and unjust," denouncing the Russian leaders "...who had betrayed socialism, as well as the centrists, 'left' opportunists, and anarcho-syndicalists, who covered up for that betrayal." Lenin's motto was "...to turn the imperialist war into a civil war." It took him four years to get his wish.

The new, internal war was made up of at least as many combatant factions as the country had left behind in Europe: the Red Army, the White Army, the Green Army, the Black Army, the Monarchists, and more, with more dead or dying either of violence or starvation. Even by their own account the Russians had thrown themselves iz ognya da v polymya—*out of the fire, into the blaze. The Russian language does not consider the frying pan to be perilous enough.*

All of which makes it difficult to envisage that, amidst all the disarray, the country was turning out a whole new generation of artists and musicians—maybe despite it, perhaps because of it. So it is equally dizzying to consider that people had the time, space, and money to patronize and enjoy the arts. Nevertheless, word had it that artists were being paid in bread, and that may have made them the lucky ones.

Just how these artists, including the young Yevgeniy Zalmanovich Kreitz, remained aloof from the combat is not always clear. Perhaps they were viewed as keeping up morale by giving voice to the Bolshevik battle cry, or otherwise by creating a new culture such as any young country needs.

Even so, an artist's life was no more guaranteed free of worries than it has ever been. In the years following the Revolution, the dangers came from another, hidden force. Musical taste at the newly formed State Committee on the Arts swung like a greasy weather cock nudged by the winds of political whim. Composers in particular walked a high-wire between fame and denunciation. They could rise high embodying the ideal of the New Soviet Man. Or they could plunge to oblivion, and starvation, under the accusation of falling into the trap of Formalism—anti-proletarian art that only those who had benefited from a bourgeois upbringing could hope to understand. Very simply, so said the Arts Committee, they had pandered to the elite. In the giddy whirlwind of the new Utopian society—not unlike the zeal (and violent zeal if necessary) of religious conversion—examples had to be made. As the Soviet State took form, the Worker was elevated to sacerdotal heights and all those who were not the Worker had to keep constant watch over their shoulders.

Kreitz saw fellow artists and musicians fall in and out of favor, and their income and status move accordingly. In some cases, they disappeared entirely from view. The meritocracy, which was supposed to be a fiction, or simply abolished under Soviet rule, was absolutely in place. Artists gained influence as they grew in favor, thereby reinforcing the idea of a meritocracy—until they fell out of favor, confirming the idea that it was a fiction.

But Kreitz excelled within the system. He played what was permitted to play at the Moscow State Conservatory. He had little or no access to the kind of decadent music that could place him or his career in any question. And he breathed passionate life into everything he played. The final years of his study were interspersed with regular visits to the stages in and around Moscow,

Petrograd, Voronezh—even at the prestigious Nizhny Novgorod Fair. Even before receiving his official diploma, his career as a successful concert violinist had already launched.

There is an old saying, "Russia has two misfortunes, fools and roads." Anyone who lived through the revolutions of February and October of 1917 could argue that those misfortunes were politics and politicians.

Russian life was an ironic existence. Almost by default, citizens found themselves both for and against everything that surrounded them. In the same vein, young Kreitz and all the Jews of his generation were as Socialist-minded as any of their countrymen. The Jews had never felt any love for the Tsar. But the antisemitic "May Laws" of 1882 had evolved into further restrictions which, in turn, made way for the *pogroms*— the state-sponsored attacks on Jewish villages, homes, and places of study and worship. Living in Moscow, Kreitz was not in any immediate danger, but neither was he blind to what was happening around him.

Kreitz had no interest in worship. He was an atheist. But, in the eyes of the government and society in general, he remained Jewish. And Jews—including Jewish Socialists—had a bad habit of disappearing, or, at the very least, falling into disfavor just that little bit sooner than their gentile comrades.

At this moment, however, young Kreitz had the wind of artistic success at his back. In the winter of 1922, the Arts Committee had chosen him to join a program to demonstrate young Soviet talent in the largest cities of western Europe.

It was then that Kreitz discovered Paris.

It was the time and place of art and literature of every stripe. *Les Années Folles* had taken root and their blossoms took the form of jazz, visual art, cinema, and free thought. A year earlier, Paris resident Anatole France had won the Nobel prize for literature. Seven months before Kreitz's arrival, British art patrons Sydney and Violet Schiff hosted a dinner at the Majestic Hotel, then on the Avenue Kléber. Igor Stravinsky, Erik Satie, Marcel Proust, Pablo Picasso, James Joyce, Sergei Diaghilev, and Clive Bell attended. Most of them were already living in Paris. Joyce had published *Ulysses* through a new bookshop called Shakespeare and Company, at the beginning of the same year.

Paris was alive with new ideas and new art. No thought was prohibited. And, to Kreitz, the ideal of the New Soviet Man was starting to look slightly less ideal.

Paris was also a Russian city. It was common knowledge that tens of thousands of Russians, often called the *Whites*, had made Paris their home after fleeing the Revolution. It was not uncommon to find former army officers and nobility driving taxi cabs around town. The running joke had arisen that it was good manners to address driver as Your Excellency, just in case. Diaghilev had formed the *Ballets Russes* in Paris well before the 1917 Revolution, but there was never any reason to settle anywhere else. In fact, the company never performed in Russia in its early years.

Within a matter of weeks, Kreitz found himself dining with the great and the good of Paris society. In these new and exciting surroundings, it did not take much effort for him to overcome his shyness, making self-deprecating jokes in French and throwing in the odd Russian word where his vocabulary fell short, only to the delight of those around him.

On 30 December 1922, the First Congress of Soviets ratified the Treaty and Declaration on the Creation of the Union of Soviet Socialist Republics. It was, of course, a treaty in name only. More like a knife to the throat of four satellite republics followed by immediate occupation and absorption into the U.S.S.R. and immediate restrictions on travel by Soviet citizens.

Five days later, a friendly French diplomat visited Kreitz in his room to explain that his musical tour was being cut short and that Soviet officials would be along, most likely within a matter of days, to escort him and his fellow performers back to Moscow—forcibly, if necessary. The writing on the wall was as clear as that written in the Treaty.

The next morning, in his own methodical style, he knocked on the doors of two fellow musicians, the only two he could trust, in their *pension* and asked to meet them for lunch.

After breakfast, he explained to the manager behind the desk that he would be vacating early. The gentleman nodded solemnly and said nothing. Kreitz donned his jacket and winter coat and walked to the ticket agency of the *Compagnie Générale Maritime* in the First Arrondissement. He walked slowly, turning around fully every few minutes to see if any faces in the crowd repeated themselves. In his best French, he made his needs known to the agent.

From there he made his way to *Au Rocher de Cancale* on Rue Montorgueil, a large, noisy restaurant near the well-populated Les Halles—easy to blend into the crowd. At lunch he explained his plans to his companions and, in keeping with his wishes, they had brought the names and addresses of acquaintances upon whom he might intrude.

After many good wishes from his colleagues, though none of them joyful, he strolled to Gare Saint-Lazare. It was a half-hour walk but his violin and suitcase were light, he was in no hurry, and he could ensure that his path was known only to him. He continued to look around as he walked, again to check on his company, but also as one does when they are saying goodbye to a place for a long time.

He would have loved nothing more than to stay in Paris for all time. But the French embassy official had made clear to him just how tenuous his ties were. Word was already out that new Soviet foreign agents—first from *Cheka* and, later, the GPU—had infiltrated the city an effort to bump off the free-thinking Whites who, by dint of their very presence in Paris, were giving the new Soviet Union a bad name.

Add to that, even in the flush of existence—the thrill when you know you have survived the explosion—Paris was still reeling from the war that came *this* close to ending more than just all wars, but civilization as we knew it. The Great War had been replaced by a hodgepodge of punitive and senseless treaties. Allied General Foch had called it "an armistice for twenty years," and he turned out to be liberal in his forecast. In the meantime, Kreitz performed in concert halls that were either under construction or reconstruction. It would take more than a lick of paint to reverse the devastation that northern France had sustained. Despite all his love for Paris, Kreitz knew it was time to head to the Land of Opportunity.

He took the next available train to Le Havre, a six-hour trip. He found a simple but clean hotel not too far from the harbor and, the next morning, boarded the *SS Espagne* for Havana. There were no crossings direct to New York City in January. Anyway, the likes of the *SS New York* and *SS Paris* were far beyond his budget. Another concern: carrying a Russian passport directly to New York would require him to pass through Ellis Island, and he wanted to avoid any eventuality that could result in his being turned away. He traveled second class—less expensive and less conspicuous.

The *Espagne* was an older ship. It did not fare well in the winter seas and neither did he. For the first four days he remained shut in his room, which he shared with a Cuban businessman—an agreeable enough person but who did not bathe as often as Kreitz would have preferred. Nevertheless Kreitz confined himself to quarters unless he had to venture out to the toilet or dining room. From his tiny cabin he could stare at the wild waves and vomit out of his tiny porthole just as much as his body commanded.

Gradually, the temperatures warmed and the seas calmed, and everyone in Second Class drew a collective sigh of relief.

On arrival in Havana, under instructions from the people at the ticket agency in Paris, he followed the crowd in the harbor to a passenger cruiser bound for Miami filled with raucous American gamblers. From there he found the sleeper train to New York.

Yevgeny Kreitz was twenty-four years old. He was accustomed to asking his parents and friends about career moves, but there was no time to be young, anymore.

Austrian immigrant Artur Bodzansky (later Bodanzky) was conducting the Metropolitan Orchestra at Town Hall in Manhattan. He knew of Kreitz, met with him, and asked him to stand in for a violinist who had not lived up to his commitment. Kreitz would have two months to learn English, learn how to use the BMT, IRT, and IND subway lines, and brush up on the Mendelssohn Violin Concerto.

The concert was well received, better than he expected, perhaps because he seemed to have come out of nowhere (and, more or less, had) and more invitations followed.

Pierre Monteux had arrived in New York shortly before Kreitz though it had not been his first visit. He was eighteen years Kreitz's senior and had built an august reputation as conductor at the *Ballets Russes*. On arrival in New York, he was called upon almost immediately to conduct the Boston Symphony. He received word of Kreitz's performance and, just a few months later, invited him to play the Brahms Violin Concerto at Symphony Hall in Boston.

Impresario Sol Hurok—of Pogar, Chernigov Governorate, and who had fled Russia before the 1917 Revolutions—collected Kreitz into his stable of geniuses within a matter of weeks of that performance. Within a year, Kreitz's name had become common knowledge in musical circles and beyond. And, not long after, the United States Government offered citizenship to the newly styled *Eugene* Kreitz.

}

FIVE YEARS LATER and three miles north of Boston's Symphony Hall, Nicola Sacco, a shoemaker and night watchman, and Bartolomeo Vanzetti, a fishmonger, were executed at Charlestown State Prison. Both were Italian immigrants and both were vociferous members of the anarchist movement. They were convicted and executed on trumped-up and almost certainly faulty charges of murdering a night watchman at a local shoe factory.

Practically every European capital saw mass demonstrations in protest of their imprisonment and hoping to prevent their death.

Young Kreitz was not blind to the events, but he felt no threat, no sense of alienation, from the growing distrust of foreigners. Of course, there were those who hailed from countries harboring political sentiments different from anything American. But the United States had welcomed him—made him their own, even. He was not a radical of any kind. If anything, he had developed a powerful devotion to his adopted home.

There was nothing to worry about.

}

IN 1946, THE SOVIET government awarded composer Dmitri Shostakovich the Medal of the Order of Lenin. One year later, Democratic senator from New York, Robert Wagner, awarded Eugene Kreitz the Congressional Gold Medal for "achievements that have had an impact on American culture, and likely to be recognized as a major achievement in the recipient's field long after the achievement."

I CONTINUED TO make deliveries for the delicatessen, and no longer—or not only—for record money, because I had discovered a vast collection of free music just waiting for me. By some act of magic, my mother's record collection appeared out of thin air and bequeathed itself to me. Never mind that it had been there since the beginning of time. Never mind that my mother had shown me the collection when she played the different versions of the *Pathétique*. It had not been there for my purposes until I was ready to find it. Until that moment, anything that was my mother's was either unimportant or inapplicable. All I had to do was make it mine. And, of course, offer it on permanent loan back to her, should she ever wish to use it.

She had assembled a system that placed J.S. Bach next to Count Basie, Dave Brubeck before Max Bruch, Chopin ahead of the Chordettes, Jascha Heifetz with Dick Hyman, Glenn Miller and the Modernaires in the middle near Nathan Milstein, George Shearing with Henryk Szeryng, and Paul Whiteman and Henryk Wieniawski at the end of the line.

Some of it remained a mystery—why the musical *Oklahoma!* came between Ruggiero Ricci and Franz Schubert. Or why *Show Boat* neighbored Witold

Lutosławski, and *West Side Story* stood just after Luciano Berio.

One thing was clear. There wasn't modern or classical or jazz. There was only music.

My mother had a few LPs of violin and piano duos. One record, called *Your Favorite Recital and Encore Pieces,* contained a piece I did not recognize—not by the name, anyway.

Johann Sebastian Bach, Charles Gounod
Ave Maria — *"Méditation sur*
le Premier Prélude de Piano de S. Bach"

I listened and understood. How could I have missed this? It was my old monkey piece, the Bach Prelude in C with the addition of two measures repeated at the beginning. Plus violin.

I could do this.

{

"I've brought you a gift. I hope you like it."

Mr. Kreitz's eyes shot to my hands which were empty.

"Goodness. I can't remember when someone last gave me a gift." He tried to look behind me. "Where are you hiding it?"

I smiled slyly. I held up my hands like a television magician and wiggled my fingers. He cocked his head to one side, an elderly puppy.

I decided to end his confusion and sat down at the piano.

"Ah. It's *in* your fingers!"

I stared at the keyboard for a moment and prayed that these fingers would not let me down. Not too fast. Hear the melody. Remember the emotion. I started to play the Bach C Major Prelude, but I only played the first four measures, then I repeated them. I looked up at Mr. Kreitz and did my best to smile.

"What are you doing?" Something changed in his voice. I did not have to look to see his displeasure. *Keep playing*. He'll hear how nice it is.

I kept the smile on. "Well, you asked me to play something. I thought I could ask you to play, too." *Keep playing*. "You said your... that you didn't have any accompanists anymore."

"I said they were dead. I didn't say I couldn't find any."

"Well, you can find one, now." I realized, a little late, that my response did not exactly match his remark. *Change tack.* "C'mon. It'll be fun."

"Michael, what do you think you're doing?" His voice was angry now.

I stopped playing, right in the middle of the phrase, but I did not look up at him.

"Do you think that, just because we've started having these little chats, you think I'll dig out my fiddle and play kitsch music with a teenager? Do you expect me to perform like some dancing dog again because one more person offers to be my accompanist?"

I wanted to tell him how much I had hoped to hear him play. I wanted to tell him how much I had learned from him. How my music had changed just by talking to him.

I put the fallboard down and slid out from behind the piano.

"I'll go."

"Michael."

Don't talk.

"Michael." Big sigh. "I'm sorry I shouted."

Just leave. Show your strength.

"Michael, let me explain." He squeezed his forehead. *"Blyat!"*

"You know, Mister Kreitz, you actually might be happy if you picked up your violin now and then. What else do you have? Your old records? Your radio? You think it's enough just to talk about music? To ask why we love music? To ask why we love to play music but not actually play music? It's *music*! It's not silent in your head, it's aloud, in your hands. You were the one who said to me…" I tried to put on his voice. "'*How sa-a-ad that your friends don't play music.*' Because it's a great thing to play music. It *is* great, only you don't do it. You just talk about it. But you can't just talk about music."

I wanted my face to show anger. I wanted it to say, *Am I all you have?*

And now there was the feeling of sickness. I had broken the rules. You didn't talk back to old people and you certainly didn't tell them what to think. I wanted to run, but what would he think then? If I believed so strongly in what I said, why did I feel like throwing up on his carpet? I held still and hoped the feeling would pass.

I wanted to believe this was an idea he'd done his best not to have. I wanted to believe that he was turning this brand-new idea over in his mind. I knew he'd never say anything as amazing as *You know, you may be right*, but I hoped he would. I wanted to be right even more than I wanted him to play music with me. None of this was happening.

"I'll see ya 'round."

ʒ

A WEEK LATER Mr. Kahanah picked up the phone. Phone calls were usually delivery orders. It was a quiet day so I was happy to hear it come in.

"Mister Kreitz, how are you! You didn't have to remind… Oh… OK… Two? Sure thing."

Mr. Kahanah looked like he was trying to identify an odd smell.

"He ordered two pastrami and chopped liver sandwiches. Is that a little strange?"

I shrugged, but I recognized the invitation. I didn't have to tell my mother I wouldn't be home for dinner. It was almost always something out of the freezer on the weekend.

An hour later we were apologizing to each other. Still, I could not let it go.

"Mister Kreitz, you gave up the one thing that made you happy."

"And exactly how do you know it made me happy?"

I tried to say something, but nothing came out instead.

"You think it was all fun and games? Dragging myself from city to city? Playing second-rate halls. Making nice on… on *pridurki* because that's where my money was coming from? Is this what I was doing it for?"

"So, are you saying there's only one way to play music? Either you're at the top or you can't play at all?"

"As a matter of fact, that is what I'm saying. There is *only one* way to play. What do you expect of me? Where do you expect me to play after hearing cheers in Carnegie Hall and the Gewandhaus?" He walked across the room and looked out the window, away from me. "Don't you think I've had invitations from the likes of the Far Rockaway Cultural Association? Can you not understand what kind of a degradation that is? You know, I've played with the Podunk Philharmonic or whatever they were called. That was enough humiliation. A lot of us do that, but it's not a good sign for your career. As soon as Carnegie Hall sees you playing with the Lower Slobbovia Symphony, they write you off." He thought for a moment. "They wrote me off." He looked back at me, drew a deep sigh, and tried to smile. "You know, you shouldn't worry about me. I was at the top of my game for thirty years. I played for another five, just to play. But there's such a thing as quitting while you're ahead. Jascha Heifetz is still playing and I'm not so sure he should. Fritz Kreisler, the greatest violinist of his time, traveled to hear the eleven-year-old Heifetz perform. After hearing him Kreisler said, it was time for everyone to break their fiddles over their knees. I'm not sure he would say that now."

I was looking for something to say. Even one word. And there it was.

"Mister Kreitz, what about the fun?" This time I hoped I could surprise him, but he just shook his head.

"Nope, there comes a time when it just isn't fun

anymore." He thought about that. "Do I miss it? Sure, I guess I do. Who wouldn't miss being on top of the world… no matter what you do? But there comes a moment when you just have to count your blessings."

Later that evening I found myself wondering. What makes a person famous one day and not famous the next?

{

THE TEMPO OF DAYS accelerated. Kids returned from summer camp and there was a flurry of parties before school started. I knew I wasn't popular but my guitar was. There was clearly something more attractive, or compelling, or magnetic about music coming from a living person connected to an instrument than from a disembodied machine. I didn't understand why—I still don't—but it gave me the chance to play music. I had to play, more even than before. Anything would do.

I tried to be a good friend to my friends. Most days, though, I was anxious to see what surprises the piano held for me. And as much as I liked my Richie and Donny and the rest, they could not tell me anything nearly as interesting. I was isolating myself, I knew it, but I didn't really care. It was a question of substituting one loneliness with another. One solo with another.

School was the moral equivalent of war—an unpredictable consecution of fear and boredom that averaged out to a generally thudding odium. The emotional version of a headache. Something to overcome or, if possible, ignore. If school had taught me anything at all, it was how to pay just enough attention to pass my tests with a grade that would keep my mother from sitting me down for a talk.

My real week went from piano lesson to piano lesson. Over time, the lessons themselves evolved into discussions. What the best way was to play a passage. What the composer meant by *forte* or *allegro* in a particular spot. We talked about why Glenn Gould sat so low at the piano and whether I should do that, too. I could not pull down on the keys the way he did. I was used to pushing down on them from above and that seemed to suit Lily's and my taste. We thought about how his style differed from that of Horowitz or Rubinstein. We worked more and more on ensemble pieces. Sometimes I took a lesson with another advanced piano student to play four-hands pieces. Sometimes I played with a young violinist, the student of another teacher in Lily's building.

I was devouring pieces, practicing before school and again after dinner. To spare the neighbors I closed the piano lid, placed the music lectern on top, and covered the piano with some old blankets that we never used.

When I got too tired to practice, I took out another record from my mother's collection, brought it to my room, and played it, and played it, and played it, and played it, and played it, and played it, and played it until I knew it. The next night, I took a different record. For a while I went through the list alphabetically. If I didn't like the picture on the front, I'd move on to the next one. Or sometimes I didn't want to hear Baroque music, or Modern music, or Romantic. Finally, and though it would take months, I made my way through the entire stack.

To Lily's credit, she never once asked me to play *"Für Elise"* and, to this day, I can't play it.

❧

WHEN THE SPALDEEN got too cold to punch, punchball made way for touch football on the playground. I took part but wasn't very good. I was also worried about hurting my hands. Every time someone suffered a jammed finger, I'd excuse myself and head home to practice.

Beethoven and Schubert were jealous of my time. They demanded more attention than any other music, and much more than I gave my punchball buddies. But the music returned to me a friendship that I found nowhere else. I tried to see composers writing to me from a place far away in the world, far away in time, in a mind that was made to create. How had Beethoven managed to bring the Moonlight Sonata into this chamber almost two hundred years later? I tried to imagine gray matter expressing sound through ink on paper. I was fascinated by the fact that they spoke German yet, when they wrote, I understood everything. What had the old man said?

THE TREES PREPARED themselves for sleep. The streets awoke from their summer lethargy to create the city we think of when we think of New York City—the one that pulses the yellow blood of taxi cabs flowing along arteries of asphalt.

I scheduled my lessons so I would have enough time to walk from school to Lily's apartment. The traipse up Eighth Avenue—through Chelsea, Midtown, the Garment District, Times Square, past the musical theaters, the movie theaters, shlock shops, porn shops, and record stores—all helped get trigonometry out of my head, where it had never been welcome.

There were frankfurter stands if I took the route along the Park. I could jam down a Sabrett, with "the works," and only add a minute to my walk. There were chestnut stands suspended in a sour miasma that mingled with steam gushing from manholes and subway grates. There were car horns. And there was a man in the intersection of Fifty-Seventh Street and Broadway, dressed in a suit and tie, directing traffic, while no one took any notice.

❧

"OK, I think it's time for you to start on Beethoven's *Pathétique*."

I looked at Lily, just a little confused. She had never introduced a piece this way. *Time to start?* I remembered my mother describing the *Pathétique* to me months ago. I remembered thinking it would be hard to play. Maybe Lily thought the same.

All I could do was give my signature shrug. "OK."

"But I want to tell you a little bit about it, first."

I tried not to shrug twice.

She collected her thoughts. "The *Pathétique* is one of those perfect pieces that music gives us once in a very long time—sometimes decades, maybe even centuries. And, by *perfect*, I mean it gives us everything music *can* give—the physical, the mental, the emotional. It surprises us with turns of phrase and changes of key. It introduces themes that are new and different but all linked elegantly. And, at every turn, it makes us think and feel."

She turned to the piano. "The whole thing starts with this great, big C Minor chord." She played it just as loud as she could, leaning her entire back into it, and let it resound. "It can sound angry or sad, resigned or entirely hopeless. And I, the player, get to determine that by how hard I strike it, or how long, or how much silence I leave after it—or all of that."

She continued to hold the chord down, and she held the sustain pedal down.

"If you look at the sheet music, you'll see there is nothing—no notation—that tells us to hold it for longer than a beat and a half. Beethoven gives us nothing more than that. But some performers will hold it for as long as it needs to let it die away, no matter how long it takes. Others use technical tricks that force the piano to make it decay." She looked under the piano—more, I think, to show me where to look—and put her left foot on the damper pedal. "And others will just let the sound drop until it matches the next chord—also C Minor."

She played the next five chords much more softly.

"Some music historians point out similarities between the *Pathétique* and pieces by Bach and Mozart that are in C Minor and have some similar figures." She played the first few notes of a Mozart sonata by heart. "The fact that they're in the same key doesn't interest me much. But obviously Beethoven was listening to them. That doesn't surprise me at all."

I nodded to keep her going.

"What I find more interesting is that, in the third movement, there is a syncopated fugue that reminds me of one of Bach's Two-Part Inventions."

She paged back to the third movement and played it. I think she actually knew it already because she hardly looked.

Now I was curious. "Can you play the Bach for me so I can hear it?"

She looked at the ceiling. "Uhm... let me think. It's Number Six, I think."

She played the first eight measures. She was right. I could hear the similarity. And she played it note for note without the sheet music.

"He also includes a miniature Classical sonatina that sounds more like Mozart. Mozart, by the way, had only died a few years before this. Anyway, by including all these pianistic figures—the *tremolando* octaves, the Mannheim Rockets, the Alberti bass—" and she played each one as she went along, "Beethoven is saying *thank you* to his predecessors. But the piece begins and ends with this... this force that shouts *only I am Beethoven.*"

She stopped and checked me. "How'm I doing?"

"Actually, you're scaring me a little."

She smiled. "That's OK. This piece deserves some respect."

"More than others?"

She smiled again. "Yeah, I think so. That's because there are so many different ways to play it. Some people hear Beethoven, the Classicist, and play it in the Classical style. They stick to a strict tempo and structure. Others hear Beethoven, the Counter-Classicist. They'll use the music to show everything he left behind—the four-square creations of the Classicists before him. And others hear Beethoven, the Pre-Romantic, to show what his music will finally become—an entire period of Romantic music filled with *pathos*. That's where it gets its name, by the way. In case it wasn't clear, there's nothing pathetic about the *Pathétique*. It was never Beethoven's idea to call it *pathetic*. His publisher came up with that idea. The first movement has been called angry, dark, even tragic. But, not pathetic. Even at its saddest moments I can't imagine it arousing pity."

I hadn't even made the connection.

She sat back from the piano and sighed. "OK, then, I'll leave you to it." She smiled—different from any smile she had ever given me before. It carried calm. Complete trust. Confidence without expectation.

I think I knew at that moment that I had arrived—somewhere, at least.

❧

Practice was hell. I went to the Lincoln Center Music Library and listened to five different versions, and they were all completely different. They really were Classical or Romantic—or both. It was also the only time I had ever seen hundred twenty-eighth notes in a piece, basically as fast as you can drag your thumbnail down the keyboard. Yet some of the performances took them slowly, almost as if to say *I'm not going to fall into your trap. I want to hear all those notes*. What was truth?

Beyond that, the notes were not harder than other pieces. But there was something about it that was not written on the paper. Something demanding.

The *Pathétique* is full of surprises and *aha* moments. One thing that struck me after practicing it (for the hundredth time) involves one figure, one combination of notes. About two and a half minutes into the first movement, Beethoven drops in a secondary theme— four notes: B-flat, E-flat, F, and G-flat. They tell us we have moved from C Minor to the key of E-flat Minor. Just four notes which he repeats with all the necessary adornment. It is beautifully terse in a way that Beethoven does so well.

But then, at the start of the final movement, he repeats it. Exactly the same figure. Only, now, it is back in the original C Minor. The same four notes, just a little faster. When I first heard it, I thought, *what a funny coincidence*. Of course it is not a coincidence. It is a concurrence. There is nothing coincidental about it.

I decided to learn the second movement, the quiet movement, first. It's the easiest one to learn because it's slow, and I needed a little success to get me started. I also loved it from the first note.

⁊

I CAME HOME to find the house dark. There was a note on the piano lectern.

THERE'S MACARONI AND CHEESE IN THE OVEN
CALL LILY

I had never called Lily on the phone. I didn't even know her number but I knew where to find it. We had a metal clapper next to the phone in the living room, a thin metal box that contained all the numbers we needed. I pushed down on a hard plastic clip at its base and the box squeaked open on a spring hinge. Inside lay a stack of foxed and furled sheets notched away on one side to reveal letters of the alphabet, plus *Mc* in between M and N. After some paging back and forth I came across Lily's name and number. I pinned the lid down with my index finger and kept my thumb next to her name. With my free hand I picked up the receiver and dialed the number.

"*Darling.* Thanks for calling back. You remember the Bach *Largo* we worked on? I think it was ten-fifty-six."

"Sure, I know it."

"Well, can you just give it a run through? I'd like to play it with you again next lesson."

"Uhm, OK… Why?"

I could hear the smile in her voice. "It's better if I tell you when you're here."

The amicable tone had been meant to allay my concerns but did nothing to diminish my dislike of surprises. I simply had to assume that she was pairing me up with another pianist. But why all the mystery? And why this piece? I finally decided I was about to meet a famous pianist, or hoped I would.

I went to the piano and found a tall and motley stack of sheet music in repose behind the lectern—a geological record of all the music I had worked up. I had forgotten about some of the pieces. I had forgotten how much I had done. There was something in the chronological list that spoke of my obsession to consume sound. Strange also to think that, half a year ago, it had taken me more than a month to chew through a single piece. Until recently, I was doing two *Kinderszenen* at a single bound.

I pulled out BWV 1056 and realized—or remembered—that I only had the second movement, the *Largo*. It was the only part we had worked on. For me though, it was its own piece, even with its cliff-hanger ending. I had become used to that. I didn't have Lily's piano part but wanted to remind her about how to play it right. I put the record on, the first I had bought with my deli money. I duplicated the first few chords from the string section. Their *pizzicato* made the accompaniment almost diaphanous. The closest thing on a piano is *staccato*, but that doesn't work. It would be pointy and unpleasant here. So I tried to create something that falls between *staccato* and *legato*—hard but not impossible.

I let the movement play through and it launched into the third and final movement, the *Presto*. It says something very different. It's urgent, almost angry. It takes itself very seriously. In any case, it's everything that the *Largo* is not. Still, something was missing. I realized I had not heard the first movement—called *Allegro Moderato*—maybe not ever. It had *everything* to do with the third movement. At once it was a complete piece of music and I was reminded of my mother saying, time and again, "I hate when these radio stations play just one movement of a symphony. It's not the whole story. It's like hearing someone say 'And then I went to the store.' What's the point of that?" The first and third movements were a beginning and an end. The second movement, in the relative major key, was the third wheel. The story—the whole story—is one of an angry soul taking a moment out to contemplate beauty. I had only played the pretty part. It was beautiful, but there was more.

{

A FEW DAYS LATER I made my way to Lily's apartment. The weather was showing the other side of the City's personality—the unrelenting cold. Lily's weekly glass of Coca-Cola made way for a cup of hot cocoa, which I took greedily.

Lily greeted me with her customary fanfare—in fact, more even than I was used to—and realized quickly that the extra helping was for the benefit of a gray-haired woman sitting on her couch. The woman remained seated but smiled brightly at me. She wore what my mother called a suit, though there was no shirt or tie involved. She also had something on her head that looked a little like a tiny woolen kettledrum. I imagined it had been all the rage ten years earlier.

Lily saw that we had already caught each other's eye and said, "There's someone I'd like you to meet."

I walked over and she stood and offered me her hand to shake. Or, not so much her hand as the top of her wrist. I wondered if she was expecting me to kiss her hand. I twiddled her fingertips.

"How do you do Michael, I'm Mrs. Pattingall. I'm here for the Turtle Bay Cultural Society. I've heard quite a bit about you from Lily." She moved her eyebrows in time with her words.

I didn't much like this woman being here. I didn't like her being in my territory. I didn't like it that they had talked about me. But I imagined that I looked stupid just staring at her.

"You have?" was all I could manage. Wait, they had been talking about me? I think I remembered to close my mouth.

"Well, we have our own little orchestra." The woman giggled. "I mean, we're not the New York Phil or anything, but we hold our own." I smiled politely and waited. Finally the silence became uncomfortable. She cleared her throat. "So, once a year we like to feature *young* talent. At our Spring Concert."

I very nearly said, *Do you want me to come see them?* More silence. Finally, she blushed.

"Michael!" Lily blurted. "She's asking you to play!"

"She is? You are?"

Lily burst out laughing. "C'mon let's play the Bach."

"Well, but I only know the second movement."

"I know. We'll worry about the rest later."

We moved to her two pianos nestled into each other, hip-to-hip.

I sat down and started playing "Comin' Thro' the Rye" in F Major, just to warm up my fingers. I looked up and could tell Lily was giggling to herself. She turned to the woman who had seated herself on the couch.

"Suffice it to say that's not the Bach."

I had played at eight of Lily's year-end recitals, which I hated but put up with. I had played for Mr. Kreitz, which had made me nervous. Right now, I saw before me a thousand strange faces expecting me to perform. I felt paralyzed.

Lily gave me her loving smile.

"I seem to recall you had a strong feeling about the tempo," she said. "Why don't you count us in?"

I played the first chord to get the feeling and closed my eyes to hear it. I then looked at Lily and bobbed my head gently, four times.

We started in and the first thing I noticed was that Lily had gone back to her old, romantic way of playing her part. I felt annoyed at her not remembering the way I liked it. Was this what performance would be like? Playing with orchestras that didn't play the way I wanted? I checked Lily's face to see if she was testing me, but she was scrutinizing the sheet music. I played my part louder, more staccato, to try to send her a signal. *Play it this way*. Finally I just had to ignore her if I would ever get through the piece.

The room did not darken as it had in the past. Crickets did not come out to sing to me from across the mountain lake. There were just the notes and the pianos and the woman sitting across the room. Lily and I played correctly. We kept in time and we were well balanced. And there was no feeling. It was only correct. It hardly felt like music. I became aware that there was a wrong way to play this piece—without thought, without heart—and, how quickly it just became a row of notes and nothing else. I was betraying my best friend.

We finished and the woman stood up, smiled broadly, and gave a rapid clippity-clap of her hands. She came over to me and offered me her knuckles again. "How nice! Well, I certainly hope you'll join us in April. Can I have your phone number?"

Lily broke in. "I think it's better it we handle it through me,"

"Ah, of course," the woman tried to screen her surprise. "The proper channels, of course." Her eyes went back and forth between the two of us.

Lily walked her to the coat rack, thanked her, and let her out. She wheeled around and looked at me with a hint of triumph on her face.

"So! Whaddya think about that?"

"Well, I didn't think we sounded very good."

She laughed. "No, we sounded like shit. But, *hey*, you've got your first gig, man!"

I thought about that. Was I supposed to wear a tux and tails? Throw the tails dramatically over the back of the piano stool? Bow to the conductor with a long lion's mane on my head, like in the cartoons?

Did I even want to perform for an unknown audience?

"Why didn't you want me to give her my phone number?"

"Let's keep the music stuff with your music teacher." I needed more. "Your mom…" She was weighing her words. "Trust me, it's better this way."

Before I could ask, she turned her back and headed to her jumble that was a bookcase and, after some searching, pulled out a thin booklet of sheet music. She handed it to me.

"Let me have the *Largo*. Here's all three movements."

I looked at it and remembered, not so long ago, feeling horrified at seeing so many notes on a page.

Everything was happening a little fast.

"Am I going to need a suit?"

"You don't have a suit?"

I made a face that said, *When do I ever wear a suit?*

She made a face back. "Yeah, you're gonna need one."

"For one performance?" I almost said *one lousy performance*, but thought twice.

She smiled. "Well, I guess we'll just have to find you more gigs."

</

I CAME HOME AND found my mother in the kitchen, near the front door. I said nothing and dropped my schoolbooks at the foot of the piano.

"Lily called. She said you're going to play for a community orchestra."

"Yeah. I guess."

"She said you need money for a suit."

"Lily says I need a suit. I guess I need a suit."

"Was this your idea? Performing?"

"How would performing be my idea?"

"Honey, performing is everyone's idea."

"Well, this was Lily's idea."

Silence.

"Turtle Bay. Very hoity-toity." Her voice remained flat. "I'm going let you and Simon eat by yourselves this evening. I'm going out with some friends."

"Sure, OK."

"I've already put ten bucks on the table before I forget. You could try Crazy Marty's. They're pretty good for the money. You know, where we buy your school clothes."

"You can't come with? I don't know what to buy."

"I'm just so busy these days."

She came into the living room and shouted, "Simon, I'm going. Dinner's on the stove."

Her eyes grazed over me and she forced a smile. "See you later."

When my mother was not home for dinner, Simon

and I put the television on the dining table and watched "Andy Griffith" or "The Beverly Hillbillies" or "Dick Van Dyke" or "The Man from U.N.C.L.E." or "Bewitched" or "Candid Camera" or "Gomer Pyle" or "Get Smart" or "Gilligan's Island"—or all of them—each one ever so slightly more mind-numbing than the last. Dinner was two individual Chicken à la King Pot Pies with carrots and peas, each in its own disposable aluminum-foil baking tin.

I don't know what my mother, or much of America for that matter, would have done without the food technology that the Second World War had brought about. Just about everything edible in our house was either frozen, canned, or freeze-dried. And, the counterpoint of easy-to-prepare foods and easy-to-digest television harmonized perfectly. They required no effort on the part of the human body and mind.

During one of the commercials, I asked Simon to help me buy the suit. When we were younger, he had enjoyed playing the older brother and I hoped I could dredge up some of that old sensation. After a heavy sigh, the insistence that it could not take too long, and some complaint from him about "that mother of ours, never around unless it she gets something out of it," he said to meet me at Corvair's on East Fifty-Ninth Street. He refused to go to Crazy Marty's because they had no style. I looked down at the clothes I was wearing. They had no style?

}

TO CALL CORVAIR'S a beehive would have been an insult to bees. It was overcrowded and understaffed, and the shop assistants, if there were any, were uptight and out of sight. The Young Gents department, when we finally landed upon it, turned out to have exactly four suits that fit me, and two of those—one tartan, one Kelly green—helped to simplify the choice. At Simon's insistence we bought the nicer of the remaining two—charcoal gray, *faux* sharkskin, costing twelve ninety-five including tax—even though it exceeded my budget. Simon chipped in the extra two ninety-five and muttered something about getting the excess back from "our cheap-ass mother." He also treated me to a can of Scuf-Cote, another thirty-nine cents, so I could paint over the scrapes in my black school shoes. We agreed that I could get away with my one of my button-down school shirts. He would lend me a tie.

"Hey, Simon, I really appreciate it. I owe you one." I realized how uncool I sounded.

He looked unimpressed. "You realize you could have done this by yourself." Not angry. Just making a point.

I shrugged to hide the fact that I didn't agree.

⁊

SOMEHOW THE NEW suit made things real in a way that Lily's prophecy had not. When we got home I put it on and walked around the room a few times. I glanced at myself in the full-length mirror glued to my closet door each time I made the circle. Simon instructed me to practice: Unbutton the jacket when you sit down, button the jacket when you stand up. I sat on the edge of my bed and tried it a few times.

The room was terribly warm. I opened my window as far as it would go to let in the winter air.

With the suit still on, I pulled out the Bach record and put it on my record player. This time, I listened to the piece from the beginning. When I first learned it, I had only listened to the second movement, the only part that mattered. I noticed, perhaps for the first time, that there were other pieces on the record, but they were not of any interest. Not right now. I played the Bach all the way through on the record. It was eleven minutes long. There was another piece after it but I did not want to hear it.

I lifted the tone arm and put it back to the beginning. I noticed my hands were shaking. I had heard that, when people thought they were going to die, they saw their lives—their past—passing before them. Right now, I saw my life yet to come passing before me, but it did not feel like life. Not like my life. I had never known what to expect. I hadn't really thought about it. But I really hadn't considered this. My palms were damp. I could feel thousands of people watching me—far more than could ever fit in a concert hall. It was a concert hall that went on forever. I was subjecting myself to a life of judgment. Of inspection. I felt, just a little bit, like vomiting. What if that happened during my performance? When I was in third grade, a fifth-grade boy punched me in the face. Just in front of my ear. It didn't leave a mark, not on the outside. But it left me feeling helpless. This was the only thing that came close.

I put the record on and listened to it again. And then again. And then again. And then again. And then again. An hour and a half later, I took the suit off, hung it in my closet, and put my dungarees and tee-shirt back on. I did not want Simon to see I had been wearing the suit all this time.

I went to the piano to get the sheet music, brought it back to my bed, and read along as I played the record another five times. I noticed that Glenn Gould had made some additions to the written score. Added a trill or an arpeggio to a phrase where a wind instrument might be able to sustain the note but a piano could not. It never even occurred to me that such a thing might be allowed. But then, if everyone played the exact same notes for the exact same length of time with the exact same dynamic, there would be no reason to have different people playing the same music. Just get a machine to play the piece the way it was meant to be played. That was the point. That was how you made a piece your own. But how far could you go? The Byrds had completely reworked Pete Seeger's "Turn, Turn, Turn" and Dylan's "Mr. Tambourine Man." Made different songs of them.

Could I go that far with this?

I made marks in pencil on the score in a few of the places where Gould had embellished on the original. Or was this just one transcription?

I headed to the piano with the music. Simon was splayed out on the two-seater in the TV corner reading *Raise High the Roof Beam, Carpenters.*

"I'm going to be playing for a little while. Hope you don't mind." It felt correct to be extra solicitous after the favor he had done me.

He didn't look up from his book. "So, what else is new?"

For all the strides I had taken in the past months, written music on paper still looked like balloons on sticks getting pushed around the page by squiggles, arcs, dots, and arrows. I wondered if I would ever learn to sight-read the way my mother did. I imagined it to be completely liberating to read music as I was able to read words on a page. Just see notes and play them. Right now, there was only one way to do it.

I took the first movement at one eighth its normal speed, the right hand only, except for the places where the melody drifted into the left hand. So many sixteenth notes. And the four flats did not make it any easier. I had to stop and redo, stop and redo, stop and redo. At this moment I could not imagine mastering this piece, and I could not even think of playing it in front of a hundred people. I did not dare think there might be more than that.

§

AT MY NEXT LESSON, I took Lily through what progress I had made. It did not feel like much to me but she was kind and patient. She pointed out that Bach had used few, if any, dynamic markings. Until the Classical era, it hadn't really occurred to composers to add loud-and-soft or fast-and-slow, unless it wasn't completely obvious. So it was up to the performer—up to me—to decide how to add dynamic range, where to play in time or add *rubato*. We listened to her LP and, as it played, she made markings on my score—an extra line before the bars where I had to play by myself and wrote *Solo!* above it, and *Tutti!* where the orchestra reentered. She played a few phrases adding extra expression to hear what they would sound like.

I also heard, immediately, that Lily had a different recording of the piece—faster and sharper than mine. I had loved her recording all those months ago, but I had now heard mine so often that I could not enjoy this one anymore.

"Who's playing?" I tried not to wrinkle my nose.

She looked surprised at the question. "This is Sviatoslav Richter. Why?"

"Oh, nothing. I have Glenn Gould. It's just, well, pretty different."

She waited for more.

"I dunno. Gould plays the first movement slower. It sounds more—what's the word—important or something."

"Maybe *maestoso*?"

"OK, but, well… What's the right way to play it?"

She smiled. "You tell me."

I had been working on the *Pathétique* when everything changed. We decided it would be better to abandon it so I could concentrate on the Bach for the spring concert. For my debut. Even as I became more familiar with it, the faces of the crowds in my fantasy remained unchanged. No one shouted *Encore!* There were only people regretting their decision to come hear me. And my regretting to play for them. The only faces I could see were showing a mixture of pity and disgust. There I was wading through a morass of flat, emotionless non-music.

I had to eat before practicing because I lost my appetite afterward.

Lily advised me to practice wearing the suit and that made it even worse. Finally, she suggested that I go back to the Beethoven but then I worried about not learning the Bach well enough. I needed to know the notes completely so I wouldn't have to think about them— only concentrate on the feeling—and that only increased the terror.

Practice became an egregious mix of nausea and the compulsive need to go back for a second helping.

To my amazement, I actually learned it.

ʒ

I SCANNED THE Yellow Pages to figure out where Turtle Bay was. There was a Turtle Bay One-Hour Cleaners on East Fifty-Sixth Street and a Turtle Baygels on East Forty-Third. I had never been there. Then Lily instructed me to report to a high school gym on East Fourteenth Street—just off Stuyvesant Town—at seven in the evening, three weeks before the performance. Turtle Bay was too expensive to harbor its own rehearsal space. I was to knock loudly if there was no one at the main door.

To my relief a gray-haired man approached from the opposite direction just as I did. He was fortyish, or sixtyish.

"You must be Mike." He smiled and held out his hand to shake.

I blushed and nothing had even happened yet. "I actually prefer Michael." I smiled back.

"Well, then, Michael it is."

I knew it was my turn to say something, I just did not know what.

"Charles Rigsdale." We shook hands and I remembered. I was supposed to ask him his name. "Call me Chuck."

He reached into his breast pocket, pulled out a tiny key ring, and let us in. The door slammed behind us and echoed the length of the school corridor. He found a light switch that sent a march of fluorescent tubes down the hallway.

"How's the practice going?"

"Uh, OK, I guess. My piano teacher warned me that everything would sound different with an orchestra."

"Oh, is this your first time? First performance?"

I just assumed he knew that. "Yeah, I hope that's OK."

He chuckled. "There's a first time for everything. And everyone. You gotta start somewhere. I just thought you'd have played it with your school orchestra. Where are you? Juilliard? Mannes? Manhattan?"

I tried to get used to the idea that everything he would ask or say was going to embarrass me. "Actually, I just study with a private teacher."

"Really?" He clearly had to think about that for a moment. "I wonder how Jean—how Mrs. Pattingall— found you."

"I mean… I've played it on two pianos with my teacher. And I've done other ensemble work with other students."

"Well, we'll have you up and running in no time."

I said nothing.

We took a turn and found ourselves at the doors to the gym—identical to gym doors in a thousand high schools across America. The bank of light switches was just where it was supposed to be. The gym bore the faint smell of sweeping compound and sweat. Folding chairs and music stands were assembled in a semi-circle at the far side of the basketball court, two chairs to a stand, with space for a conductor's podium and a piano at the hub.

The piano was an industrial-grade, pre-fab console, stained light brown, covered with cigarette burns and coffee-cup rings. I lifted the fallboard to see that the keys were equally stained, or worse. Someone had drawn a circle in blue ballpoint on the Middle C. Another hand had crossed out the piano's brand name inside the fallboard and written, in marker pen, *NOT A STEINWAY*. I played a few chords. It sounded pretty much as it looked. I glanced over at Chuck. I tried not to look disgusted.

"Yeah, sorry about that. I guess you're used to better."

I considered a sarcastic answer and then just shrugged.

"Well, I sure am," he said. "I'll see if they have a better one in their band room for next time, but I can't make any promises." He chuckled. "I mean, this *may be* the better one from the band room."

A loud knock echoed from the outside door.

"That'll be our doorman—well, the concertmaster, actually. We take turns manning the door for the other orchestra members." I looked around the room. There were about twenty chairs. "I have to let him in. Back in a sec."

The nausea returned. I tried to play the first few measures of the second movement, still my favorite, except that my hands were shaking visibly. I heard the two men chatting far away. Then footsteps back to the gym. Chuck reappeared in the gym.

"The concertmaster will open the door for the rest of the people. Anyway, why don't you and I go through the piece before the others arrive? I can get an idea of how you like to do this—what kind of tempos you like, loud and soft, and stuff."

"I guess I more or less follow Glenn Gould's timing. He does my favorite version."

He smiled. "Oh, very modern of you. In that case, we might sound a little romantic for your taste."

I thought of Lily. So they were listening to the same things.

I laid my hands on the keyboard. "I like to do it about…" I played the first three measures.

"Oh, man, that's really slow—for me, I mean. What's that—about sixty-six?"

I looked him and then at my hands.

"Do you mind if we pick it up just a little? Maybe to seventy?" He sang a few measures and conducted in time. He snapped his fingers as he went. It was faster, but not as fast as the guy on Lily's recording.

"Yeah, I guess so." I wasn't entirely ready to give in. "My teacher calls my style *maestoso*."

He thought about that for a moment. "OK, I get it. But just a little faster. I don't want the orchestra to drag… if it's all right with you."

No one had ever asked my opinion. I could only shrug and nod.

"Play it again? Give me an idea of what we're going to do?"

"Can you give me your tempo again?"

He tapped four times on his lap and I started playing. He made some notes in pencil on his score as I went along. I thought of the first time I had touched Mr. Kreitz's piano. How awful it had sounded. This one was not so much out of tune as just hard to play. It sounded as if someone had stuffed a towel down the back. Some keys pushed down with no resistance at all. One key played two notes at the same time. I did not say anything.

And now I was thinking about Mr. Kreitz. A *real* musician would refuse to play this piano. A *real* soloist would insist on his own tempo.

Musicians started filing in, first one at a time, then in groups of twos and threes. Most went straight to their chairs, took out their instruments, and started warming up. A few came over and introduced themselves. Chuck looked like a proud uncle.

Finally, when everyone was seated, he stood up on the podium.

"Hi, everybody. Happy New Year to you all. Everyone have a good Christmas vacation? We've got our young soloist here for the spring concert. He's quite a talented young man by the sound of things."

I didn't know whether to wave or bow. I just smiled as best I could. I tried to ignore my desire to throw up.

"Right. For those of us who did this—what, four years ago?" Chuck looked at the concertmaster, who nodded. "We're gonna slow this first movement right down—go for that *maestoso* sound." He side-eyed me quickly and smiled.

Some of the musicians leaned their heads together and murmured.

"Not bolshy, not uppity. Just a little this side of… *serioso*." He lifted his hand, without the baton, and sang the first few measures, punching the air in time with his voice. He added a heavy accent to the first note of each measure. "So when we get to the second movement, the

Largo will sound that much more tender. Yes?" He looked around at the group.

I scanned the faces of a few of the violinists. They looked underwhelmed. The terror in me rose.

"All right, let's do a dry run just to hear how it sounds. Ready, Michael?"

What choice did I have?

He straightened up, lifted his chin to see the back row, and tapped the air with his baton in time.

I laid my hands on the opening notes—middle F in the right hand, low F in the left hand.

"One, *and...*"

By the fourth measure, I had made so many mistakes that I had to stop. I wondered if my hands would stop shaking.

Chuck rapped on his music stand three times out of tempo and held up his left hand. "OK, everybody, false start. Let's take it over. And a little more punch on that downbeat, please. Give it a little *sforzando*." He was shifting the blame. It was for my benefit, but it did nothing to shift my embarrassment.

I looked to my left at the concertmaster who stared straight ahead. His second chair, a young woman, gave me a nod and a look of *it's all right*.

I had not thought at all about how to prepare for this moment. This was not performing. It was not one of the recitals I had ever done for Lily. I was not playing for relatives. I wanted to blame the piano but knew where the problem lay. My heart would not even pound in time to the music. My ears were blocked. The orchestra sounded like it was coming from another room. I was glad that I had memorized the music because my eyes would not focus properly.

We started again and made it through to the end of the first movement. I was exhausted. After about fifteen minutes, and what felt like an hour, we got through the second and third movements. I had hoped to feel less nervous as we went along, but my heart was still pounding. I imagined I would never stop feeling nervous.

I excused myself, found the Men's Room down the hall, and considered vomiting into the toilet but was afraid someone would come in. I went to the sink and dashed my face with cold water to try to staunch the sweat. I looked up, into the mirror, eye-to-eye, with The Fraud. He would follow me back to the gym. To the concert hall. And the next one after that. Tag along with me throughout my life.

I tried to avoid the gaze of the musicians passing my way as the rehearsal broke up. A few said something to the effect of *good work* or *sounded great* as they passed, but I knew they were covering up, embarrassed to say anything else, ashamed to tell the truth. If you can't say something bad, don't say anything at all.

Chuck waited for the musicians at the front to leave. He turned to me, shrugged, and shook his head. "Man, that is one piece-o'-crap piano." He looked at me. "You gonna be OK?"

I shrugged back. I tried to chuckle, but it came out as a squelched yelp. I hoped I wouldn't cry. I looked at the keyboard. "Yeah, it's pretty bad, but I didn't help things."

He thought about that. "Listen, man, you were nervous. That's OK. You can use that energy. Drive it into your fingers. And, hopefully, a better piano will help things. You'll be fine." He leaned in and punched my shoulder.

We walked out in silence.

I came back, thankfully, to an empty apartment. I went to the toilet and vomited heartily to eject all the fret, the disgust, all the bad notes—the entire experience, if possible. To eliminate the ignominy of being a child. What is the purpose of showing people off for no other reason than that they are young? Why should anyone be thought special only because they are young? What good is that? On some terrible date, the wunderkind finally stops being an object of fascination and turns into one of pity.

The vomit made space for a layer of sweat that bore the smell of panic. I got into the shower and stood there until the water had pounded away the odor and the humiliation. I hadn't practiced enough—that much was true—and wondered if I ever could. How much practice was enough? I would have three weeks, including one more rehearsal, to get it right. Was that enough? At this particular moment, though, I only had to find a way to hide from myself.

⸱

I NEEDED SOMEONE to blame for the abomination that had been the rehearsal and Lily was the obvious miscreant. I hated being dependent on her for what was most important to me, only to discover she had duped me into doing something I did not want.

I found myself shaking, whether in anger or fear, as I approached her door. It was not logical. I needed help now more than ever. I could not figure out my own feelings. I could not feel anything. Or I felt everything.

Lily opened the door with a big smile but lost it the moment she saw my face. She turned silently, went to the kitchen, and got the hot chocolate waiting for me on her kitchen counter while I hung up my coat.

She handed me the mug. "So… what's up? You look like the cat that ate the poisoned canary."

"Lily, whose idea was this?"

"Uhm… you wanna give me a hint what *this* is?"

"Because it sure as shit wasn't mine." I had never cursed in her presence before, and it came out so easily. I wanted to scream much more at her, just for the sake of screaming.

Awareness came to her eyes. "Ah, OK, the performance."

I wanted her to know I was onto her. She had hoodwinked me. Not given me any choice. Yet, all that came out was, "I was terrible."

Lily nodded slowly. "So, now I assume we're talking

about the rehearsal, because I don't think the performance is for a couple of weeks. So… what? I pulled a fast one?"

"Well, that's how it feels." It did not come out as angry, but as miserable. I was, after all, the victim.

She took me by the hand, led me to her couch, and we sat. She looked at me and thought for a moment. "How long have you been coming here?"

I wasn't finished being angry yet, but it seemed a fair question. I just looked at my feet. "Since I was seven. Like first grade."

"So, what, five years?"

"More like six."

She smiled. "Sorry, six. How long did your brother have lessons with me?"

"Simon had lessons?"

She threw her head back and laughed out loud. "Yes, for two lousy years. And I don't mind telling you I wasn't sorry when he stopped."

Simon had skipped two years at school. He had cool friends. He succeeded at everything. How could he not do well at music? How could no one have told me that he'd had music lessons?

Lily wasn't waiting for me to process this. "You? You, I would've been sorry to see stop. Even at age seven. Even then, I could see something happening— mistakes and all." She slapped her forehead overdramatically. "My *god*, all the mistakes. I didn't know one kid could *make* so many mistakes." She was smiling. It actually sounded a little funny. "But, I could also see there was something in there. So, when you were done botching the piece, when you finally got on top of the music, you transformed. And you transformed the music. But I also don't mind telling you you've taken your good old time to get serious about it. It's been waiting inside there for a while. And, what, a year and a half ago? Two years if I'm generous. It finally popped out."

"It?"

"It. You. The musician. You know, a lot of kids would be thrilled to hear that they're talented. That they have something special. But then there's you. You'd rather die than hear—or, worse yet, know—you've got something special. So I have to be the bearer of bad news." She leaned back on the couch and stared at me. "Listen, become a professional musician. Or don't become a professional musician. I really don't give a shit. I mean it. Really not. But, *please*, don't ever ignore the music in you, because that would be a damn shame. I mean *really* a shame. You don't wanna play the concert?" She shrugged. "Too bad. Too bad for them. Too bad for you. I've got another kid—more than one—who would be very happy to play."

"You do?"

"Of course I do. What, are you nuts? I've got lots of kids who want to play. *Can* they play? I mean *well?* I got kids who are well-practiced. They've really got some chops." She leaned in at me. "But do they have the *talent?* Not really. Not like you, anyway. But they *want* it. Can you play? You're damn right you can. You've got the chops *and* the talent. But if you don't want to…"

I didn't know if I looked lost, but I felt lost. "Lily,

what am I supposed to do?"

"How the hell am I supposed to know?" She threw her hands in the air. "Don't ask me, because you won't like the answer." She stood up and shouted at the room. "This… this *investment* you've got in being regarded as the underachiever." She looked at me. "Whose feelings are you gonna hurt if you succeed? Do you think we, the adults of the world, will expect too much of you if you do too well? What would happen if you played a great concert? Would the sky fall?"

I had not even thought of these questions, but something about them hurt.

"I mean, are you really asking me, or do you just want me to say *That's all right, you don't have to play.*" She put on a syrupy voice for extra effect. I felt embarrassed at the sound. Belittled. Humiliated. Angry that I felt humiliated. But, that was clearly what she wanted. "Or maybe I should say, *No, Michael, I insist that you play. You have no choice.*" She pounded an invisible table.

"Stop. Please." I was trying not to cry.

She sat down and squeezed her eyes closed, trying to squeeze something away. "I'm sorry. This is out of place. It's just… you've been playing so well for the last— almost a year, now. I'm just worried that your old habit is gonna rear its head again. I'm afraid that you'll decide you can't do it. That you need to show everyone around you that you can't." She sighed. "Listen, are you *really* asking me?"

Was I asking? Did I want to give her the power to decide my future?

She put her hand on my shoulder. "Michael, if you

don't play, no one will know and no one will care. No one will even say, *Remember that kid who came to one rehearsal and then didn't come back?* No, they'll truly forget you—for better or worse. But, if you don't play, *you'll* never know. You'll never know how it would have sounded, or felt, or looked." She thought for a moment. "OK, that brings up the other question. Did I trick you into this? Did I *cajole* you? I guess I don't know the answer to that one. OK, maybe I acted a little hastily. Maybe I want people to hear what a great pianist you're becoming."

I tried not to squirm.

"Then, yes, guilty as charged. Maybe I got ahead of myself—or yourself. Very simply, I think you could be a great performer. In that case, you gotta start somewhere. You gotta start sometime." I was trying on too many ideas at once. She examined my face. "So, are you asking my advice or not?"

I nodded, but I could not meet her eyes.

"Then, I think you should play just this once, so you can say you did it. So you'll know you did it. So you can say you didn't back out. So you'll know what it feels like. Is it nice? Is it not nice? If you don't play, what will you know? What will you know about yourself? Does that sound like an idea?"

I nodded, though I didn't know if I was agreeing to play or just to the idea of playing. It was still not real.

She stood, took my hands, and pulled me up from the couch. We walked to the door.

"But this week? Don't play the Bach. Play something else—something you know and enjoy. Play the

Pathétique. Just as long as it's something else." She took my coat off the hook and handed it to me. "Michael—" She was considering her words. "Is this about your mother?"

The question shook me physically. I could not decide if it came as a complete surprise or if I had been expecting it all along.

"Are you afraid of hurting her feelings because you might just be better than her? I know your mom a little. More than a little. She's got a competitive streak to her. She was a damn good pianist in her young years. And, if I do know her, she'll want you to succeed—just not too much. But you can't take care of her forever. At some moment in time, you'll have to be your own person. You have to be your own musician."

My mind scrambled in all directions to find something it knew. If these were new ideas to me, why did I recognize something?

"Now go home. That's enough lesson for one day. Go on. No charge."

I put my coat on and she followed me to the door. I was trying to figure out whether I felt loved or rejected. Praised or ridiculed.

"Do you really want me to come back next week?"

She threw her arms wide open and stood on her toes. I leaned down to hug her. She pulled me close and whispered in my ear. "Always."

All week, I couldn't let go of the idea that Lily had tricked me, maybe even bullied me, into continuing with this performance. If it wasn't my idea, why couldn't I say no?

MR. KREITZ AND I continued our Friday afternoon chats, but I never got around to telling him about my upcoming performance. Or, rather, I managed never to tell him about my upcoming performance. It was not entirely clear to me why I avoided the subject, particularly of something that figured so large in my life. I knew I did not want to force him into the public eye and, if I told him, I imagined he would feel compelled—obliged—to come see me perform. I really did not want to hear him have to say, *I'm sorry, I just can't go out in public anymore*.

I wanted him to be proud of me. I wanted him to tell me I had done well. I was even prepared to hear his criticism, as hard as that might be for me. Lily had already said she would come—offer tips if necessary. That seemed normal.

But there was something wrong about inviting him when I had not even considered inviting my mother, and she in turn had shown no interest.

I think I would have been more surprised if my mother *had* turned up. Maybe she was waiting for a formal request from me, but that did not seem likely. She certainly hadn't dropped any hints. Simon had complained that she never did anything for us unless it was in her interest. I did not understand. He made it sound like this was something new, as if he had known her as a different kind of mother earlier on. I certainly had not. It was how she had always been. Her scarcity in our lives was not all that different than that of our father. The only difference was that we could see her doing it. Our father's absence might be more consistent, but hers was no less predictable.

At some level I realized it was not really up to me to decide if Mr. Kreitz could or could not come.

I finally devised a plan that would solve everything—to include him and not include him all at the same time.

The Friday after my first rehearsal, I brought my Glenn Gould record and the sheet music for BWV 1056 to his house. I would just have to be careful not to tell him more than was necessary.

"I'd like to listen to this with you. I'm playing it four-hands with my teacher," I said as I came in. No lies so far.

He picked up the album cover and examined it. "Ah, a wonderful piece—Bach at his best. And Glenn Gould! I've certainly heard about this young man. Apparently he's all the rage. Shall we give it a listen?"

He took it from its sleeve and put it on his turntable. I had played the record so often, I think I even knew where to expect the crackles in the track. He looked through the sheet music while the record played.

He lifted the tone arm at the end of the first movement, straightened up, and thought. "Well, that's a bit slower than what I'm used to, but he makes it work." He looked at me. "So, tell me what you hear."

That was not the question I was expecting, if I was expecting a question.

"What I hear?" What had Chuck said? "Well, it

sounds… important. Serious."

He thought about that. "Almost urgent, wouldn't you say? In that case we might want to write *pressante* at the top."

Urgent. I liked that.

"I'm asking because, as I guess you've noticed, Bach gives a speed indication at the top for the second and third movements, but not for the first."

"Well, I did see that, but those things don't really mean a lot to me. I've just been copying his speed."

He smiled. "And you could do a lot worse." He was quiet for a moment. "Can you play it for me on the piano?"

I should have known he would ask that. I could have prepared myself for… what? I was about as prepared as I ever would be. I had practiced the thing almost to death. My mother had said there was even such a thing as practicing too much but I was not willing to believe that.

"Uhm… sure. With the record?"

He made everything on his face frown. "I don't think that's necessary. It's you I want to hear. I know how the rest goes."

"Only the first movement? Not the rest?"

"No, let's start here."

I smiled. "Too bad. I like the second movement the best."

"And the second movement is beautiful. But, first impressions are most important."

I shrugged and nodded in agreement. He handed me the booklet and I took it to the piano, though I didn't need it. I sat down and, as Lily had directed me, I rested my hands on the keyboard and waited for the music to come.

I leaned into the piece. I kept my staccatos short and sharp and I made my left hand talk to the right. The room grew dark and the piano keys were all I could see. I waited for the soft passage to come and was careful not to hurry the crescendo—stretch it as far as it would go. The piece said *This is important stuff.* It said *Listen to me because this is all there is.*

Three and a half minutes later, I was able to breathe again. I did not look at Mr. Kreitz. I was still listening to the piano, which continued to resonate into the room.

"Michael..." His voice took me by surprise. "Michael, that was very good."

It was the last thing I expected to hear him say.

"Really?" I wished I had not said that. It sounded so childish.

He chuckled. "Really-really."

"You've clearly given this a lot of practice, and a lot of thought."

I wanted to tell him about the performance, about the fiasco of a rehearsal, about Chuck and Mrs. Pattingall, about everything. But I had made myself promise. There must have been a reason for that.

"Can you give me any advice? About the piece, I mean."

He thought for a moment. "Try to think less. That's all I can really say. Think less, feel more. But that will come with time."

᷾

A WEEK LATER, Lily opened her door for me.

"You still have that look on your face."

I said nothing. I came in and hung up my coat. "OK, how do I bow?"

She laughed out loud and walked to the piano. "Fair question. You stay here." She turned around about five feet in front of the piano. "OK, the stage manager, or the conductor, or *someone* in the wings will say *Go!* Walk toward center stage. Come on, do it. Shake the concertmaster's hand." She held up her hand and I shook it. "You know who the concertmaster is?"

"Yes, Lily, I know who the concertmaster is." It gave me the chance to look at her like she was stupid.

She smiled. "Just checking." She walked over to the side of the piano. "Shake the conductor's hand." I went over to her and shook her hand again. "Now, go to the piano, stand with your left hip next to the piano keys and your left hand on the beam. There, at the corner. The piano bench should be right behind you. Now, look at the audience and count to two, look at your toes and count to two—*c'mon, man, do it*—look at the audience again and count to two. Now sit down at the piano, close your eyes. Michael, *close your eyes*. Put your hands on the keys, but only if you want—if it helps. Now, hear the music in your head. Hear it? OK, when you can hear it clearly, look at the conductor and nod. He'll be watching you for the sign."

"Do I need to smile?"

"Not if you don't want to. Just try not to look terrified."

"What if I can't hear the music?"

"Then stand up, nod to the conductor, nod to the concertmaster, and go home." I considered that. "Michael, when has that ever been your problem?"

I shrugged.

{

CHUCK MET ME at the front door, sporting a broad grin.

We talked about the New York Mets, who we agreed were terrible, as we headed down the hall to the gym. We talked about the Yankees, who we both loved. We talked about everything but music.

I entered to find a real piano—black and everything. It was the puniest grand piano I'd ever seen, shorter even than ours at home, but it was far grander than what I'd played two weeks earlier. It was even reasonably in tune.

Chuck saw my surprise. "Turns out they had this here the whole time. We had a violinist performing last year and a clarinet the year before that, so I didn't really know what they had anymore. But I told 'em we'd stop renting the gym if they didn't come up with the goods."

A loud knock echoed from the outside door.

"I'd better get that. That'll be our next designated doorman"

He headed back out and down the hall. It seemed like the right moment to get to know the instrument. I played the Middle C and its neighboring B-flat. It sounded good—much better than the last one, anyway. It echoed through the empty gym and came back to me with a friendly sound. In those two notes, I heard the second movement of the Beethoven *Pathétique* and started playing. It is the sound of pure serenity. I forgot everything around me. That was always best—to forget. To join with the music. To fall into the piano.

The second movement is the embodiment of tenderness though it is in no way mushy or sentimental. It even has some urgency to it and, in that sense, it is just like love. I gave it all the appreciation and gratitude I had. In return, it held me close, gave me its beauty, showed me its appreciation. It turned down the lights and cooled the room.

After about three minutes, the movement returns to its opening theme followed by a natural pause. I lifted my hands to hear the notes resound.

I was met with the sound of twenty people clapping and smiling. Someone gave a loud whistle. When had they come in? How long had they been there? What had they been doing? What had I been doing? And now they were applauding me. Chuck came up behind me, put his hands on my shoulders, and spoke quietly in my ear.

"Everything's going to be just fine."

In fact the rehearsal did go *just fine*, which was to say it didn't go wonderfully—just well enough. I still made a few mistakes and we still disagreed about the tempo. I always seemed to want it faster when they wanted it slower and the other way around. We had to keep stopping to discuss things.

After about forty-five minutes, the orchestra took a break to smoke and talk. I had brought a bottle of soda and an opener. Chuck came and sat across from me in the concertmaster's chair.

"How's it going?" He smiled warmly.

I shrugged. "Yeah, OK, I guess." It seemed like the right moment to be non-committal. Not say how relieved I was after how poorly the first rehearsal had gone. Not say I wasn't happy about the tempo differences.

We stared at each other for a moment. Each giving the other the chance to speak. I was able to wait longer.

"Hey, didn't you tell me you've done some ensemble playing?"

"Sure. Why?"

"Well, because you sound like you're accompanying the orchestra. Only, you're not an accompanist. You're the soloist. Let them accompany you. *Show 'em who's boss.*"

I think I stared blankly at him.

The silence went on too long and he started to look uncomfortable. "For one thing, play louder. For another, tell me I'm full of shit when I tell you what speed to take the piece."

I REMEMBER ABSOLUTELY nothing about the actual performance. Lily told me it went well, or well enough. I looked nervous and I played a little too softly. But it was fine.

I only wish I could remember it.

}

A FEW DAYS LATER, I came home to find a note on the piano lectern.

I'M OUT THIS EVENING
ASKED RUBIE TO MAKE DINNER FOR YOU
SHE'S EXPECTING YOU ~6:30

Simon was gone but that was no surprise. It gave me less than an hour to practice, wash my face, and put on a fresh tee-shirt. Practice didn't go well because I kept stopping to check the wall clock behind me.

Finally, I bounded up the stairs to Rubie's apartment, waited at the top so she couldn't hear me panting, walked calmly to her door, and gave it a *shave-and-a-haircut* knock (without the *two bits*). I could hear her walking to the door. She opened the door wide and gave me a smile to match.

"Well, you're Peter Prompt."

I turned to look at one of her paintings hoping she did not see me blushing. The canvasses were still on their easels. Still unfinished.

"Come on in." She turned back to the kitchen and I was able to watch her all over.

Rubie was, very simply, stunning. She always wore the latest fashions without looking showy-offy. This evening she was wearing a mini dress with giant polka dots, all of which accentuated the length of her legs. She was barefoot and I could see her go-go boots leaning against her reading chair. Her eyes were almost black and she wore a large swath of purple eye makeup up to her eyebrows.

I entered the room quickly, hoping to catch a scent in the bubble of air she had just occupied. And there it was. Just the faintest mix of perfume and perspiration.

I watched her from behind. She had her hair pulled back with a large clip, which bared her lovely neck. She caught me staring, grinned, and turned back to her kitchen. I watched her skin—caramel, coffee, molasses. The hollows of her knees were especially captivating. I could be happy just curling up in the hollows of those knees.

"Hamburgers OK?" she called.

"Sure!"

"Mashed potatoes?"

"Yeah!"

"And your mom said, *'make something green,'* so I made a salad. Hope that's all right."

"That's fine." I hated salad and didn't care. I adored her and she was completely out of reach. I could not imagine what I would do with her even if I won her heart. She was twice my age. She was twice my *you name it.*

"Hey, your mom said you played a concert."

"Yeah, I did."

"What did she think?"

I wanted to shrug but she was not looking at me. "I dunno."

"Well, she went to see you play… I mean… Didn't she?"

"Uhm, she couldn't come."

"Oh… OK." She kept her eyes on the stove and stopped trying to converse.

Jazz was playing on her hi-fi set. It sounded crazy. A saxophone winding and swooping and swirling around the piano, bass, and drums. Not really talking to them. Just kind of off in its own world. I didn't particularly like it, but it was probably good jazz because Rubie was playing it. It was just over my head. I watched her again and another jazz song, "Teach Me Tonight," came to mind.

Meat hissed. Pans knocked. Even the food smelled better here.

"Tell me what I can do to help. Set the table?"

"Got it covered." In fact, the table was already set and the salad bowl was in place. The dining table was all of six steps from her kitchenette—a stove, refrigerator, and sink with cabinets above.

"Just have a seat. I can't cook and talk at the same time."

I sat in a chair across from her boots and listened to the jazz some more. The piano, bass, and drums were clearly listening to each other. The sax just was not paying attention. I preferred Dave Brubeck. He was nice and tidy and, even with his unusual rhythms, at least everyone was playing the same thing.

"What's this music?" That sounded rude. "I mean, who's playing?"

I thought I heard her say *train*.

"You mean like, 'Take The "A" Train'?"

She giggled. "Nope, I mean like John *Col*trane."

She brought two plates to the table, fully laden. We talked about the summer heat. Adults seemed more bothered by the heat than kids. I had noticed that before. Adults sat in front of electric fans all day in the summer while my friends and I were out playing in the full sun.

We talked about the school where she taught and my upcoming school year. I don't remember much about it. I just wanted to keep her talking so I could watch her and listen to her voice. The food was good. I didn't want it to end. We cleared the table. I offered to wash the dishes and she refused.

When we were about to sit down, I asked her to play the song that the jazz musician had written for her. I remembered my mother expressing her doubts about this particular piece of history. "But don't let the facts get in the way of a good story," she had added.

Rubie seemed especially pleased at the request. She went over to her stack of records, pulled one out, and put it on her turntable.

"It's called 'Ruby, My Dear,'" she said while laying the tone arm on the disk. The change in spelling was not evident in her speech.

We listened in silence. The music was, well, OK. I actually found it a little boring. It had some interesting chords, but the sax player just sounded tired, maybe even bored. And the people were missing notes—the pianist especially.

She lifted the tone arm at the end of the cut. I put on my happy face. "Nice!" I couldn't think of anything else to say and she was clearly waiting for a response. I hoped I hadn't hurt her feelings. It was her song, after all. I watched her.

A smile crept onto her face—not so much happy as sly. She walked back to the record player. "I've got one for you."

She put the record back in its sleeve, returned it to the shelf, and pulled out another.

"This is called 'Coming On the Hudson.'" Thelonious Monk. She laid the record down, lowered her head to bring her nose level with the disk, and lowered the tone arm with care onto a track in the middle.

The music started and, at once, I felt disoriented. Out of place. My whole head hurt while she looked so relaxed, almost exultant. How could she look so calm, so happy, when the same sounds made my head ache? She sat back in her overstuffed chair and watched me. Trying to listen to this music felt to me like trying to breathe on Mars. There was nothing for me to recognize, there was no foothold. The chords were all over the place. I had learned my music theory. I understood tonal attraction. C can go to F or G or D Minor or A Minor—but these weren't even *chords*. I couldn't count any meter. The saxophone said, *this is some kind of melody*. The drums said, *this is some kind of beat*. But what melody? What beat? Without knowing why, my head wanted to count to four, but it could not. This music said, *you will not follow me*. I couldn't find a thing to like.

The song came to an end and she giggled. "That was different, I'll bet."

I tried to keep a straight face. I didn't want the

confusion to show. "Maybe I just don't get it."

She was smiling but she was not laughing at me. In fact, her face was full of love. "Maybe not. It's pretty… out-there. This record's like seven or eight years old, so it was *really* out-there when they made it. I think it says a lot that it still sounds pretty crazy."

Finally, I had to let the grimace out. I would suffocate if I didn't. "Rubie, he's playing the wrong notes."

She laughed. "You're not the first person to say that. That's the best part. I'll have you know he was aiming for *every one* of those wrong notes, and he hit every one! Monk even says *the piano ain't got no wrong notes.* Think of it this way: What's he doing when he misses a note? He's hinting at the note. He's *assuming* the note. That way, you get to hear the note you wanted to hear *plus* the one he's playing. You get more for your money."

I couldn't let this go. He just was playing the wrong notes. "I mean… I know about improvising… a little. I listen to jazz sometimes."

Her eyebrows showed her surprise. "You do? What kind?"

"Well, we have Dave Brubeck."

Her eyebrows fell back into place. "*Ahhhh!* White guys." My confusion redoubled. "Black folks play by different rules… Literally!"

"You call them *Black?*"

She sighed. "First of all, whatever names you have for *us people*, you can forget about them, right now. We're Black, OK? Enough about all that. Let's talk about the music. Let's talk about Black Jazz and White Jazz."

"So… there's a difference."

"Yeah, there sure is."

I must have still looked like I was searching for some kind of flotation device.

"The white world hasn't allowed Black people into their world. So, should they be surprised if we don't feel the need to play by their rules? They're saying—right here in this song—*You wanna play four-quarter time? You wanna play one-four-five chords? You go right ahead!* And, by the way, one-four-five was Black *long* before it was white. Long before Elvis was singing 'Blue Suede Shoes' and Bill Haley did 'Rock Around the Clock,' that was the boogie-woogie blues. It was Black music invented by Black musicians. All Elvis and Haley did was make it acceptable to white folks."

"Do you hang out with… you know… Black people?"

Rubie threw back her head and laughed. Her tiny stomach bounced up and down. " *'Course* I do, honey. I'm Black, or haven't you noticed?"

I could not have felt more stupid. "Well, sure I noticed." I tried to make a scoffing noise. "I guess I only ever see you downstairs at brunch." *Acting like a white person.* How could I say it? "We have lots of… well… Black kids at school." I found that hard to say. "You just don't sound like them."

She widened her eyes, stuck out her full lips, and rocked her head left and right. "Oh, so you want me to go all *mammy* on ya?"

I felt myself blush. Everything I said was wrong. Her face softened.

"OK, I get it. I guess you don't know me that well.

Yeah, I have at least as many Black friends as white. But it's a white world we live in."

"So… what do you do with them?"

"Michael, they're *friends*. We hang out. We talk and joke. We listen to music."

Everything I said made things worse. I had to rehabilitate myself.

"Could I come visit some time when you hang out with some of your friends? Maybe I could understand the music better if I hear everyone talking about it."

She giggled. "Sorry, honey. I'm afraid that wouldn't be possible." She looked at my reaction. "It's not *you*. It's that you're too young. We go to bars where they serve alcohol and you're not old enough."

I hated being told I was too young for *anything*. She saw my face.

"Hey, I have an idea. Next time I have some *Black* friends over, I'll invite you up for a short visit. But when I tell you it's time to go, it's time to go, OK?"

I didn't like the conditions. Always conditions with old people.

"Yeah, OK." But I made it clear I wasn't happy.

I could see ideas going around in her head. "Let me play one more number for you."

Again, very delicately, with love for the medium, she lifted the record from her turntable—I had never seen such care for a plastic disk before—slipped it back into its jacket and went in search of another. With the same ritual, she slipped the new one out holding it just by its edges and rested it on the platen. Again she brought her eye down to the record and laid the needle on a track in the middle.

Suddenly everything changed. Joy exploded from the speakers. There was this incredible marriage of voice and instrumentation. Everything fit. It exuded perfect structure and complete freedom. It was a demonstration of utter bliss. I never wanted it to end. Neither did the audience in the recording.

"This is Ella Fitzgerald singing 'How High The Moon.' It's actually a combination of two songs. Part of what she's scatting is 'Ornithology' by Charlie Parker. It uses the same chords."

"Two songs? There's another song?" Then I realized there were *all kinds* of songs in there. How did she do that? "Is that allowed?"

Her shrug said, *I guess it must be.*

"And what's *scatting*?"

"Singing without words. She's using her voice as an instrument. She's improvising—like, *scatadda-do-dah*. They say Louie Armstrong invented it when he forgot the words during a recording."

"Play the Ella song again. Please?"

She went back to the turntable and lifted the arm. The sound of the screaming audience ended abruptly. They liked it as much as I did.

"So, what's she singing in there?"

"Now *that'll* be a test of my musical knowledge." We ended up playing the song four times over.

She closed her eyes. "OK, there's 'Poinciana'... there's the old Paul Whiteman tune 'Deep Purple'... God, there's lots more but I can't catch it all."

"I only heard the Jack Benny song."

"Right, that's 'Love In Bloom.' There's the Mexican hat dance. But she also sings the lyrics to 'Did You Ever See A Dream Walking' and 'Idaho' and 'Havin' a Heat Wave.'"

"Wasn't that The Lone Ranger at the end?"

She giggled. "Well, thank goodness for The Lone Ranger. Oh, and of course 'Ornithology' like I said."

"Well, so what's *Ortho…* '? Do you have that?"

"'Ornithology?' Matter of fact I do." She went through the ritual again. This time she blew a few sharp puffs through red, pouted lips at the disk before laying it down. I wondered if I was taking good enough care of my records. Every time one developed a scratch, I'd put a penny on the tone arm to help it cut a fresh groove.

The music came on and it was wild from the start. There was a fast drum solo and then a saxophone and trumpet playing in perfect unison, much faster than Ella Fitzgerald had sung.

"And you're saying that this is the same song that she was just singing?"

Rubie waited for the melody to come around again and she sang. OK, maybe she didn't sing it as beautifully as the woman on the record, but she carried the tune well. Her voice was high and clear. Not as earthy as Ella, but she actually made it swing a little. And it came from Rubie's lips..

"I didn't know you could do that!"

She giggled. "Oh, I'm full of surprises."

♪

I STARTED LISTENING to more jazz records. I don't think I particularly liked them, certainly not at first, but I wanted to show that I was listening to Rubie. This music had to be good because so many people seemed to like it—people I admired. Hip people. I couldn't stand some of it. She had explained that these musicians knew exactly what they were playing but I couldn't completely believe her. What was the point of playing stuff that just sounded… well, wrong? Sometimes they weren't even playing notes. Sometimes they were just honking on their horns.

But I started noticing other things. The musicians I understood more quickly happened to be white. I didn't get a lot of Black jazz. Was that because I was white? White jazz seemed to be more orderly. Was that a good thing? Or were they missing the point? Or was I missing the point? Rubie said Black musicians didn't care about playing according to white rules. Was it that I didn't know what the rules were?

Sure enough, a few weeks later, Rubie dropped a note in our mailbox inviting me upstairs to join a few of her friends. Here were six Black adults… and me. I could not have felt more out of place. A kid, and white.

Jazz was playing on the hi-fi and they were throwing around names like Bird, Dizzy, Bean, Trane, Prez, Cannonball, Sweets, Lockjaw… No one seemed to have a normal name. The women's names sounded normal enough—Nancy, Sarah, Nina, Dinah, Carmen, Billie, Ella… but they didn't need last names. When it came to the white musicians, complete names were called for—Dave Brubeck, Anita O'Day, Bill Evans. Neither Bill nor Evans would do. White musicians didn't stand out. They needed more explanation.

Nobody seemed surprised to see me. Clearly Rubie had announced my arrival. She stood behind me with her hands on my shoulders. She introduced me and I waved at the group trying to look as relaxed as I could, and feeling anything but.

Just by how they were seated, I could tell that one man had the lead. Within a few turns of the conversation I learned that he was a jazz sax player. His name was Carl. I felt impressed, whether I needed to or not.

"Are you famous?" I asked and immediately felt stupid.

"Nah, I'm a minor leaguer. But I get regular work. It's good enough for now." He smiled and put on a sly face. "But I'm *gonna* be famous."

Rubie pushed me closer to the group. "Michael here's a musician, too."

Carl looked genuinely interested. "You any good?"

How do you answer that? I still don't know.

Rubie felt the pause go on a second too long and said, "Oh, man, this kid practices and practices. Morning, noon, and night."

I turned around to look at her. I wanted to say *I do?* or *Do I make that much noise?* but she had a big smile on her face so I just let it go.

One of the women—I don't remember her name—said, "Hey, I brought along this record. I wanted to know what you think about it." She was talking to Carl. The pressure was off.

After nods of agreement from the group, Rubie put it on her turntable. I sat down and we all listened to the first track in silence. No one smiling. No one looking at anyone else. No one looking approvingly or disapprovingly. It was a saxophone, piano, bass, and drums. The track came to an end and all faces turned to Carl. The record continued to the second track, which was a ballad.

Rubie laughed and said, "Well, *c'mon, man.* You know we're waiting for you to say something."

Carl shrugged. "What's the guy saying? What's he trying to tell us? I'm not hearing any real message. Far as I can tell, he's just trying to show how good he is."

Rubie saw my face. "Michael, you look like you've got a question. Maybe you can say it better than I can."

I doubted that but I was on the spot now.

"Well, but, isn't that what all musicians are doing? Aren't they just showing how much talent they have, how much they've practiced. Y'know… how good they are?"

Everyone's eyes went to Carl.

"OK. Fair enough. But, what are you gonna to do with all that talent and practice? What do you want to *say?* Why do you like one version of a song better than another one? Sure, *everyone's* playing the right notes.

It's not about talent. It's not about practice. It's about the message."

⸮

A FEW WEEKS AFTER my performance—I *think* it was at the Ninety-Second Street Y—I came home to find a note from my mother with a phone number. Nothing else. Maybe she wrote CALL first. I only knew it was for me because she had put it on the piano lectern. Usually she at least said who or what.

I reached a woman in an office somewhere. She was the volunteer librarian at the SoHo Symphony. Could I come play with them in two weeks' time? Their soloist had just dropped out. I could play Bach 1056 again if I wanted, or something else if I preferred.

I actually do remember that performance. I don't think I was very good. I was nervous. And, even when I managed to calm down, I thought it all sounded a little dead, a little timid. And something else. I didn't belong. Here I was, this new person. This kid. I didn't know anyone and here I was just elbowing my way into a group of people who knew each other, who belonged together, and I was taking over. They said they were glad to have me but I found it hard to believe.

Following that, calls started coming in—four months apart, then three, then two—from the Morningside Chamber Orchestra, the Ditmas Symphony, the Fort Tryon Philharmonic, the Long Island Sound—a smaller group. And, I could play the Bach Concerto again if I wanted, or something else if I preferred.

All these local orchestras kept asking me to play Bach and that was fine. I loved Bach and I think I was good at it. But Lily had given me a bunch of piano concertos to listen to—in preparation, or in anticipation, or just in case—and I started wondering if there wasn't a Grieg kid walking around New York. And a Schumann kid. A few Mozart and Beethoven kids. A Brahms kid. Maybe even a Liszt kid. Maybe *even* a Rachmaninov kid. But it was fine. Just a little… odd.

Over the next year, the performances got more fun to do, once I got used to the whole idea. It the game to have that kind of appreciation. I got used to seeing things in performance programs—seldom anything more than a photocopied sheet of onion skin—like *an exciting, young talent* or *a new face on the musical scene*, though all I could think was, *they don't get out much*. I was able to buy a new suit with my earnings—one that fit and didn't feel like a wetsuit. Not that I was earning anything to speak of. You don't have to pay kids much more than carfare.

I have to say I was starting to like the appreciation. Playing alone, playing for myself was good. No, not good. Way more than good. In fact, playing music—at all—was no longer a choice, any more than you can say *I'm not going to breathe today*. Music had become a bodily need. If I did not practice for a day or two, something in my head started to hurt. Where my hands once ached if I practiced too much, they now ached if I did not. But to play for people and see recognition and gratitude in their eyes, to know that something in my mind could make it through the airwaves and into their minds… This was an amazing idea. I was catching on to why people liked doing this.

Only one thing was better. Making music with other people was the best drug. Hearing sounds coming from other musicians gave me new ideas—that Surprise of… *Of course*. Here's another way to play it. And, in return, I could make my instrument talk to theirs. It tickled something in my brain—in my entire body. Everything in me started to sizzle. It was pure pleasure and it made me want more. On a few occasions I went out to a bar with the other players after the performance because it turned out they were just as buzzed as I was. I had to make do with soda while they could soothe themselves with alcohol, but I didn't mind. I just had to stop performing on Sunday evenings because I could not wake up for school on time the next morning.

After playing Bach 1056 three times, Lily and I decided it was time to venture out. We chose, or she chose, Bach's first Keyboard Concerto in D Minor. Over time we could take them all in order. There are seven keyboard concertos, depending on how you count, plus the six Brandenburg Concertos, all of which have interesting keyboard parts though they are really meant for harpsichord.

They're fun because you can play them with as few as eight people—six strings, a flute, and the keyboard—so I felt like I got to know the people a little better. The hard part is playing soft enough with a small group so you don't overpower anyone. Also, the keyboard's left-hand is the same line as the cello and it can be hard to stay together sometimes.

I could tell that Lily was especially pleased when we made it to Brandenburg Number Five because it was her favorite. She liked it because it had a little *razzamatazz*, as she put it. It is the only Bach concerto with a true keyboard cadenza—a solo part for the keyboard. It is especially nice because it sounds harder than it really is. It has a lot of sequential lines—it repeats the same passage over and over, but starting on different notes, so it sounds more complex than it is to play. It gets a lot of wows and that's fun.

Actually the fifth Brandenburg *is* hard. It's just not so much in the notes as in the feeling. The fast and slow, the loud and soft. When you start listening to those things, that's when it gets hard.

There is also a Triple Concerto, which features the first violin, the flute, and the keyboard. That one is fun because the instruments really get to talk to each other. Actually, the Triple Concerto also has a cadenza, although it's about a minute and a half long. There is also a concerto for three harpsichords, but that's different.

Actually, all the Bach concertos are meant for harpsichord. But these local orchestras operated on tiny budgets and were happy to have me play anything they could get their hands on.

Actually, the sixth keyboard concerto is the fourth Brandenburg Concerto, sort of. Different key, different arrangement, but basically the same. And the violin solo from the Brandenburg becomes a keyboard solo.

Also Bach's seventh keyboard concerto in G Minor

is basically his A Minor violin concerto. It's all a little confusing. It means you have to make sure you're playing the right one.

Plus, a lot of these things started out as oboe concertos.

Anyway, I couldn't play the harpsichord.

⸘

EITHER MY MOTHER was a strong woman or she put a lot of effort into playing the part. There was something almost mannish about her character. She talked loud and smoked and drank and cursed. She loved to argue at the brunch table with her friends about how to redeem the world—and she argued to win. But, when any of her friends would call to ask what they could contribute to the weekly gathering, she would shout, *"A man, goddammit!"* into the phone. If she was so strong, why did she need a man?

The tough-lady bit never bothered me. In fact, there was something reassuring about having a tough-assed mother. Before going into my teen years—entirely dedicated to looking like I didn't care about anything— I could be weak and she would be strong. My friends thought she was cool because she told dirty jokes. I didn't think she was cool or not-cool. As far as I knew, all mothers smoked and drank and played Beethoven. She could put on earrings and a cocktail dress and high heels and the men in her quartet would give her an amiable wolf whistle as she made her entrance. Or she could watch a Yankees game on a Saturday afternoon in a pink-flowered housecoat and furry slippers with a cigarette hanging on the corner of her mouth. It was who she had always been.

While I was the last one to notice, I was changing. I was spending less time at the playground and more at the piano. I had a reason to practice. I had something to practice. I wasn't playing some piece of crap for my grandma. I was playing for a man who had been a real musician. I was starting to understand that it had to be more than just correct. It had to be good. It was a new idea, but I think I got it. It would still be a while before I realized I was playing for me.

Something else changed. The house grew colder. My mother became quieter. Angry when I didn't practice. Angry when I did. Silent at dinner. Could it be that all my playing was upsetting her? I didn't know what was scarier, broaching the subject or leaving it unspoken.

"Sure. Why wouldn't I be OK?"

"Well, I don't know. The only time we talk is when you call me for dinner or I ask you for my allowance."

She didn't look up from the dishes. "What—you mean we used to talk? You mean I'm not bugging you enough to do your homework? Should I tell you to take out the garbage? Or do you want to discuss Kafka?"

"Mom?"

"No, I know. We can talk about Bernstein's interpretation of Brahms."

"What did I do to make you mad at me?"

She closed her eyes and sighed. The water continued to run over her hands. I had never before felt afraid of my mother.

She lifted her hands out of the dishwater and I had to push my feet into the floor to keep from flinching. For a moment, I thought she was going to throw the pan she was washing. She also seemed to be steadying herself—forcing herself to move slowly and methodically. Still, she did not look at me. She turned off the tap, bent down for the towel and wiped her hands slowly. She did not dab her hands with cold cream. Instead she leaned against the sink with both hands. I was not sure if she was holding herself up or trying to keep the whole room from flying away—and I thought it might at any moment.

"OK." She seemed to have trouble moving at all, whether sighing, grimacing, shouting… "OK, I'm not *angry* with you. Or, I'm not angry with *you*. If anything, I'm angry with myself. *If anything*? I'm jealous of you."

"What? *Mom!*"

She sighed again. "C'mon." She walked past me and into our TV corner and lowered herself—slowly, carefully—onto our flowery two-seater couch. She pulled a cigarette from a pack lying on the floor. She took the cigarette backwards in a pencil hold and tapped it a few times hard against the pack. I thought she was trying to drive the cigarette straight through the pack. Again in slow motion, she placed it between her lips and lit it up. "Sit down." I stayed where I was. I didn't want to be right next to her if she was going to start shouting at me.

"*Please* sit down."

I didn't want to but I did as I was told.

"You may not understand everything I tell you right now. I'll try to explain as best I can."

The couch was tiny but I managed to sit as far from her as I could.

"Do you think I wanted to be a music teacher when I was growing up?"

I shrugged. I had never thought of that. My mother was a music teacher. She had always been a music teacher.

"Suffice it to say that a lot of people who become music teachers didn't grow up hoping to be music teachers."

"Well, I think Lily likes teaching music."

My mother considered that. "You might be right. I think she does. But, what if someone had offered her a thousand dollars to make a record instead of teach kids who forget to practice? Which do you think she would choose?"

I had never thought about that, either. "Do you think Lily didn't want to be a teacher?"

My mother closed her eyes and pinched the bridge of her nose. "Actually that's not my point right now. Right now, I need to tell you a little about myself."

I tried not to move. I tried not to breathe.

"Michael, I'm angry about a lot of stuff these days. I'm angry about things I should have done. I'm angry about things in my life that I had no control over." She took a long drag from her cigarette and blew it out hard. It gave her the chance to sigh again. "Sometimes I think about what if my life had been different. What if…" She glanced at me and… Was she sad? Was she angry? She looked away. "What if I hadn't married your dad? I mean… What if I had been born a man?"

Something on my face told her I wasn't following her entirely.

"Have you ever noticed how many male musicians there are out there compared to females?"

One more thing that I had never given any thought. "Well, I just kind of guessed that it was man's work. Like doctors and lawyers and—"

"Exactly. Like doctors and lawyers. Because women can't do that? And what about cooks? Why are women the cooks at home, yet the chefs in restaurants are all men? Do you think men are just naturally *better* at everything?"

I felt myself blush. "I guess I hadn't thought about that, either."

She looked at me with disbelief in her eyes. Then she looked out at the empty room and spoke to some invisible person. "I can't believe I raised this kid!" She looked at me again. "Michael, are you aware that I was a good musician?"

"Huh? I think you're a good musician now."

Her face softened and she stroked the back of my head. Always a good sign. "That's very sweet but it's not what I mean. OK, sure, I know my way around a keyboard, but Horowitz I'm not." She took a drag from her cigarette. Her eyes searched the room for words. "Michael, there was a time when I was good. I mean *really* good. Concert quality. But I was missing one thing. Can you image what that might have been?"

My mind started to race. I realized she really wanted an answer from me. "You mean you didn't practice enough?" This had to be a lesson to me. "You lacked discipline?"

She smiled at the sound of the phrase which she

recognized as her own. "No, Michael. It's actually simpler than that, and it'll probably sound a little strange." She fixed her eyes on me. "The one thing I lacked was a dick."

"OK, Mom, now that's just gross."

She leaned back and smoked some more. "OK, let me rephrase that." She didn't want to smile. She wanted to be angry. "Michael, there's some big unfairness in the world. You see, not all women want to be schoolteachers or secretaries… or mothers. Some of us want to be… I dunno… bankers or stockbrokers… or professional musicians. With this new crop of female violinists coming up now, the best thing anyone can say about them is, *she plays like a man!"*

I shrugged. "Well, so why didn't you just go and do it? Why don't you do it now?"

She was silent for a long time. "Actually, that's the question I've been asking myself these days." She smoked again. "Michael, in the nineteen-fifties—and forties *and* thirties *and* twenties—ladies had babies. That's what they did. That's what we do. I mean, don't get me wrong. I'm very happy to have you and Simon. But my responsibilities have changed. I've got you now. Who would take care of you?"

I thought of telling her that she could go out and play as much as she wanted, but I didn't want that.

"And, anyway, I'm not the musician I was twenty years ago."

"You're not?"

"Remember nothing else, but remember this. If you want to be a good musician, you gotta start young and you gotta keep your chops up."

This was a day for things that had never occurred to me. She thought for a moment.

"Who's the oldest baseball player you know about?"

"Satchel Paige. He's fifty-nine!" I felt that little bit of knowledge had vindicated me… of something. I wasn't sure of what.

She laughed out loud. "OK, you got me there. Bad example."

I felt some kind of relief and was prepared to be magnanimous. "But he doesn't play a whole lot. I think Warren Spahn is pretty old and he's in his forties."

She nodded. "Thank you for that. My point is that musicians can play longer. Jascha Heifetz is in his sixties. Vladimir Horowitz, too. But they started very young and they never stopped. Horowitz doesn't perform anymore. I'm sure he practices regularly, though not the three-hours-a-day stuff he was doing when he was on stage." The smile fell from her face. "But I have stopped."

"What do you mean? You play every week with people."

She waved the remark away. "That's playing for fun. We stop and start. We think about how to play something differently. It's a fun way to play, but it's not serious practice. It's not the hard work. Not the hard practice. It's just playing. There's a big difference between practicing and playing. You know that?"

I didn't know, but I nodded anyway.

"So, I've noticed that you're practicing more. No, you're practicing *a lot* and I hear a good pianist in there. In fact, I hear a great pianist tucked away inside that head and heart of yours. I suppose I always knew it, I just didn't know if he would ever come out. Michael... I think you could be a great musician." I felt terrified at her words and I didn't know why. What did that mean? "So, all of a sudden, there's all this practicing! Don't get me wrong. I'm thrilled, but how'd that happen?"

I looked away. "Oh, you know. I just like it." Why was I such a bad liar? My friends could lie shamelessly to their parents. Here was a perfect chance to lie. To keep my secret. He *was* my secret. He was my private property but there was no way out. It didn't help that I hated lying. I hated being lied to. I hated dishonesty and now I would do anything to be the perpetrator. All I could do was shrug. Play it down. Make it sound unimportant. "I've met this old man on my deli rounds. He's just some old musician. He doesn't play anymore. But he knows a lot about music and we talk. I don't think he sees very many people."

"A lonely old man?"

"Yeah. We talk."

"Who the fuck is this guy? I mean, is he some kind of nut? For all I know he could be taking naked pictures of you."

"What? No, Mom! He's a nice old man. He was a violinist long ago. I think he's afraid to go outside, so I bring him food from the deli. He only orders meat, so Mrs. Kahanah packs a salad for him and they don't charge him for it. I bring it over and we talk about music. I guess he's lonely."

"Or maybe he recognizes a good musician when he sees one." Why did that scare me when she said that?

"Well, what's his name? Maybe I've heard of him. I know one or two musicians, after all."

"I doubt it."

"Please, I only want to know his name."

"His name is Kreitz."

She stared at me. "So… Zhenya Kreitz." Her voice had offered an answer but her face was without expression. She was always so dramatic. The dark space that her face had become frightened me.

"Uhm… I think I heard Mrs. Kahanah call him Eugene Kreitz once."

"Eugene Kreitz?" She squinted. "You never heard me mention that name alongside Sasha Schneider? Or Leonid Kogan?" She waited for a response. "*Eugene* Kreitz? *Yevgeniy* Kreitz?" I didn't even know if these were questions anymore. "*Zhenya* Kreitz?" The harder I tried to remember, the less that came to mind. "Your friend is Zhenya Kreitz? You've been visiting all this time with *Zhenya Kreitz?*"

"Mom, what did I do?" I heard my voice tremble. A minute ago she had been so happy. "Anyway, it's not *all this time*. It's been a couple of months. OK, maybe a little longer."

She got up from the couch and walked to the front door next to the kitchen. I thought she was going to march out of the house. She got as far as the door, stopped, and turned to me.

"Do you know who Eugene Kreitz is? No, obviously you don't."

I remained quiet. I knew that there was no good answer right now.

If she had been planning on walking out the door—something I had not discounted—she had changed her mind. She walked over to the record collection. She started pushing through them, a little too hard, until she found three LPs and lurched them from their spots. She paused and stared at the covers. She looked at me, walked over to the couch, and thrust them at me.

"*Eugene* Kreitz?"

I rested them on my lap and took in the photos. They were shot with strong contrast between light and dark. Some in extreme close-up, some at dramatic angles. There was a man in his thirties or forties, maybe fifties—who could tell? People looked old in old pictures. He stared dreamily past the camera, hugging a violin gently to his chest. His hair was jet black, clear to see even in the black-and-white images. This man was strong and vital. Mr. Kreitz was old and frail. I looked at my mother and remembered a photo of her as a teenager wearing bobby socks and saddle shoes, sitting on the steps of the brownstone where she had grown up. People got older. I understood that part. Even so, how could I have not seen his name or face among all these records? Was it that I hadn't wanted to recognize him here?

I was looking at the record collection as if for the first time. There was Eugene Kreitz right after Fritz Kreisler. Right before Wanda Landowska. Probably right where he had always been. Except that he hadn't, because he had not existed until that moment. He said he had been a violinist—not a famous violinist, and certainly not a world-famous violinist. My mother was a pianist. She didn't have any records. And my father's one and only record—of which there were probably ten copies in the world, if that—showed how little that proved.

Sometimes I felt like I knew nothing about anything.

❧

THERE WAS NOTHING else to say. She went to her bedroom and closed the door. I went to practice, but I could not concentrate. I could not even play the parts that asked for no thought. My fingers would not listen to me.

I walked back to the couch where my mother had left the records. I sat down next to the stack, picked them up and looked at them. Two were regular records but one of them was a three-record set. Across his photo it read, *Eugene Kreitz Plays J.S. Bach Sonatas and Partitas for Solo Violin (BWV 1001-1006)*. For a moment, I forgot how to breathe. He knew I was playing Bach but hadn't said a thing. Maybe he had nodded, but then what should he have said?

I put the first disk of the set on the hi-fi, sat on the floor, leaned against the wall, and listened. If I closed my eyes I could see his fingers punctuating the fingerboard, the bow driving and switching and darting over the strings. Every movement seemed devoted to a different emotion. This one angry, this one lonely, this one wistful, this one weightless. And there was that other thing. He knew *exactly* how long to hold each note, how hard to strike it, how much space—no matter how microscopic—to leave in between notes. All these things created the emotion I heard.

Even now, all these years later, when I hear any recording of the Bach Unaccompanied Sonatas and Partitas other than the Kreitz version, I think to myself, *they're doing it all wrong.*

৲

NOTHING REALLY CHANGED in the house—nothing I could really detect, anyway—except that I was practicing more all the time. I loved the facility that my fingers were gaining. I could command them to play loud-soft-loud-soft. Left hand loud, right hand soft. Fifth finger loud, second finger soft. Move, almost without thought, from mordent to three-against-two to trill. And then tie it all to emotion. I didn't have to think *I want this to be angry so I need to play this part...* No, sometimes angry was soft. In fact, pretty often, angry was soft.

I felt older. The apartment in which I lived felt different. A piece of me had moved out.

A few days later, at the end of a long practice, my mother peeked her head around the corner.

"I held dinner until you were done."

I startled. "Uh, OK, thanks."

"I made roast chicken. Grandma's recipe."

"Great. What's the occasion?"

She shrugged and disappeared back to the kitchen. I heard her call, "Anyway, dinner's ready."

I sat down at the table which was only set for two.

"Where's Simon?"

"He said he'd be out. Studying or hanging out with friends."

We each got two cookies for dessert. She pulled out a cigarette and lit up. She sat back and thought.

"Mike—sorry, Michael. Is there any chance I could

meet him? I dunno… make dinner for him? Invite him over for coffee?"

And my happiness turned to nausea.

"I don't think so. He hardly ever leaves his house. I don't think he likes meeting new people." *And he's mine.*

"Well, could I go with you to his house, you know, to say hello."

"No. That won't be possible. He doesn't even have his name on the doorbell or anything. He'd be very angry if I told people where he lives." *As angry as I am now.*

"Michael, I don't think you realize what he means to me—to musicians of my age. He changed my life. He changed music. I would have given anything to meet him. I… well, I'd still be so glad to meet him. I can see I've upset you but I don't think you can imagine how I feel. We're talking about my hero. Imagine for a second you could have dinner with Paul McCarthy."

"John. Girls like Paul. And it's McCartney."

She pressed her palms against her eyes. "OK, I stand corrected. But do you at least get what I'm saying?"

I had to admit that I did get it.

≀

THE NEXT DAY, I walked the three blocks to Mr. Kreitz's house as if I were walking to my death. All of my friends could just say *fuck you* to their parents—some in as many words. I could not. I could not lie. None of those things, and it pissed me off that I couldn't. I was going to hurt, or frighten, or embarrass my friend and I could not bear to do that, but I said I would and now there was no going back.

I gave my traditional knock on his door—Beethoven's four knocks in the hope that he would recognize it. *Don't be home.* But of course he was. It took him a long time to answer the door, but he did. Again, it was the expressionless Cyclops behind the crack in the door. Then that same gasp.

"Michael, how nice to see you!" He opened the door. "Michael, what's wrong?"

"Hi, Mister Kreitz. Nothing's wrong. Not really. Can I come in?"

I sat on his couch. The room seemed darker than usual, though I guessed that was just me. He sat down next to me. There was true concern on his face.

"I've mentioned your name to…" —I was going to say *old people*— "to my mother and my piano teacher and they…"

He sat back. Not quite a smile on his face. Not quite a frown, either.

"Ah. Of course." He sighed. "We never made any kind of pact. I never asked you to keep me a secret, though I suppose I probably hoped for that."

It was my turn to say something now but I didn't know what. He remained silent and waited for me to formulate a statement, a question, something.

"Mister Kreitz, who were you?"

I supposed that was exactly what he was expecting because he said nothing. He stood up. There was no joy in his face.

"Please come with me. I'll show you something."

His living room had two doors at the back. One went to his kitchen. Through there, I could see his garden. The other door was closed. He had gone through there the first time to get money for my tip. The door led to a small room with a desk. I guessed his bedroom lay beyond that. He flicked the light switch as he went in. The office was as tidy as the living room except for some stacks of mail on the desk. I looked around as the lights came on. The walls bore a long line of framed photos, each with its own, dedicated spotlight hanging from the ceiling. Even with all these tiny spots illuminated, the room was still dim. The curtains were drawn. The quiet in this room pushed in on my ears.

I looked closer and saw that the photos were all of people in formal wear. Most were holding musical instruments—mostly men, a couple of women. I saw that Mr. Kreitz was in all of the photos. In some of them he had his violin tucked under his elbow. In others, he held it by the scroll and let it dangle down. In all of the pictures, the people were smiling broadly. I only recognized a very young Leonard Bernstein but there were a few other men holding a conductor's baton.

Mr. Kreitz remained quiet as I walked from one photo to the next. I was prepared for the younger face, the one that I'd seen on my mother's records. The black, wiry hair, combed back. The confident face with barely a wrinkle. While I looked, he walked over to the corner of the room. There was a large cardboard box, an ancient cardboard box, covered with papers—more letters by the look of it, which he put on his desk. He then opened the box which ejected cardboard dust onto the floor. Silently, solemnly, he leaned in and pulled out records, as many as he could hold in two hands. He sifted through the duplicates and put one of each copy on the table. He went back to the box and exhumed another pile, pulled out the duplicates, and did it a third time. I walked over and looked in the box. There were still many more. I looked at the tall stack on the desk, lifted each one, and laid it down gently next to the stack so I could see the one beneath. Each was different. Each had a different photo and a different title. Each had his name on it. One or two had Russian writing on the front and a crude photo of a very young man. One had no photo at all. In some of the pictures, he stood smiling in groups of four or five people. Some showed him standing in front of orchestras. I recognized a few of them from my mother's collection. I felt like I was looking through someone else's baseball card collection at school. *Got it. Need it. Need it. Got it…*

I stopped after a while. I understood enough.

He sorted through the records, looked at each one, considered it. I could almost see the sound passing through the vinyl and into his mind's ear.

Alongside the solemnity of the moment, there was a calmness to his face that I had never seen. This was something he had wanted to do—to unburden himself of some of his history. By giving me these records, his past grew just a little bit lighter.

Finally he set aside six of the records, put the rest back in the box, and handed the smaller stack to me. He nodded but he did not smile.

"Take."

"I can't."

Of course, I had been waiting for him to say that, but I knew I could not take them. If nothing else, I did not want my mother to have them.

"It's OK. Play them. Don't play them. Just take them." He pushed them into my ribs and I took them.

I followed him back into the living room with the records in my hands and sat down. The part I didn't understand was what I was doing here.

"So. Can you keep a secret?"

I had to force myself not to shrug.

"I mean, not from your mother or your music teacher. They already know, of course."

I said nothing.

"I was pretty famous, once."

"Mister Kreitz…"

He smiled. "OK, fair enough. I mean, I just think it would be better if you don't go telling everyone you see,

'Hey, I know this guy who used to be famous.' I… well, I like my privacy. Do you know what I mean?"

I nodded. And then I remembered that I had come here for a reason.

"Well, here's the thing," I said and watched his face. Did he know what I was about to say? "My mother's a piano teacher. She teaches on Henry Street."

"Yes, I know the place."

"And, she performs now and then with her quartet."

His face remained neutral but he didn't look very happy, either. "Oh, so she's part of a piano quartet."

"Uh, yeah, that's what I mean." Was there any way at all to delay this? To say something else entirely?

"Might I have heard of them?"

"I don't know. I don't think so, but I don't know how famous they are. I mean… they don't have any records or anything." Clearly there was something about having records that was important. "But here's the thing." I had to steady my voice. "My mom would really like to meet you."

And there it was. He frowned and looked away. And I hated myself.

"It's just that she asked me to ask you. She said she could come here. I said no… if that helps. She just wants to have coffee with you. Maybe she just wants to be able to say that she's met you, you know, kind of the way I want to say I've met The Beatles. You're… well, you're kind of her hero."

He was quiet for a long time. I could see his eyes going everywhere. Then he wrinkled his brow.

"How old is she?"

The question caught me by surprise. It wasn't anything I thought about very much.

"Uh, forty-three, I think. Something like that. Maybe forty-five?"

His eyes opened wide. "Wow! Either she saw me when she was a kid or when I was nearing the end of my career." He watched me for a moment. "I have to tell you, I don't really like doing this kind of thing. I loved making music. I *had* to make music and so I became a musician, but I didn't really like people falling all over me. I don't think I'll like it any better now."

I nodded, but I felt sad.

"All I can tell you is you'd be doing her a big favor."

He sighed. "Well, I suppose I'm curious to see the mother of this talented child."

"Thanks, I'll tell her." *Wait, what?* "You think I'm talented?"

He tilted his head to one side and examined me. "I think you're very talented."

"But… you've hardly heard me play!"

"And that matters how?"

I did not feel flattered—only confused.

"Well, because I see these kids my age playing all kinds of instruments, like on Leonard Bernstein's Young People's Concerts on TV and they're amazing."

He thought for a moment. "So are you impressed by them or afraid of them?"

I had to think about that a moment. "I guess both."

"I don't agree. I think you're intimidated."

I tried to process that. Was that the same as afraid?

"Here's how I see it." He stood up and faced me. "All

those kids practice like mad. Practice, practice, practice, practice, practice. I'm sure of it. Maybe more than you do. No, *absolutely* more than you." He smiled. "But that's where the talent part becomes important." He held one hand under his chin, the palm facing the floor. He had his other hand at his waist, also with his palm facing the floor but rising slowly to meet the upper hand. It looked like a glass filling up with liquid. "You can practice and practice. But you can't pass the height of your talent." The upper hand blocked the lower one from going any higher. Then he raised the first hand over his head. "If you have *this* much talent and you don't practice to fill the talent," he looked at his hand, "well, that's a problem." Then he raised the practice hand to reach the talent hand, which was now as high as he could reach. "But if you have *this* much talent and reach *that* with skill, *well…*!" He smiled. I think he liked how clear he had made his illustration.

"My mom says, 'There's no substitute for talent, but there's no substitute for practice.' I think you just explained what she's been saying. I never really got it."

"*Ah*, but here's the thing. If you can be anything else at all, you should do that. If you don't *have* to be a musician, don't." There was something about that remark that hurt. "Just *don't!* Be a teacher or a doctor or a plumber. But don't be a musician unless you're prepared to give your life to it."

"So when you say you think I'm talented—"

"It means nothing." He looked at me closely. "*Nothing!* Enjoy being talented and then do something else."

"What if I don't want to do something else?"

He chuckled. "I was afraid of that. Then be prepared to give up a lot of things. *And* consider the possibility that you won't be the best, but you'll have to continue being a musician, anyway. There are a lot of people out there called *talented* and whom you've never heard of… and never will."

"But… what do they do?"

He shrugged. "A dozen different things. They teach. They do studio work. They perform anyway… just not at Carnegie Hall." I thought of my mother. "There are plenty of venues in the world—of all sizes." He looked at me and sighed. It looked like he was putting on a brave face. "So… when do I make my appearance?"

THE FOLLOWING SUNDAY afternoon, I knocked on Mr. Kreitz's door. It took him a little longer than usual to show up but he appeared. He was wearing a suit, which even I could tell was terribly out of fashion. The jacket had lapels that almost came out to the sleeves, his tie only reached halfway down his ribcage, and his trousers were pulled up much too high. Other than in the photos on his wall, I had never even seen him wear a tie and it seemed entirely out of place. I struggled with the idea of making a comment, perhaps encouraging him to dress more comfortably. Finally I just guessed that he felt most comfortable this way—as ridiculous as I thought he looked.

I realized at once that I was wearing a tee-shirt, blue jeans, and sneakers. He seemed to take no notice. As hot as it was outside, it was always refreshingly cool in this half-underground apartment, and he was perspiring lightly.

"Mister Kreitz, you look awfully warm in that... tie."

"Do I?" He scurried over to the long mirror that he had behind his front door and fussed with his clothing. The short part of the tie in back was sticking out to the side. The whole thing was all very nearly backward.

"My mom isn't really a formal person. You probably don't need it."

He looked at his image, wagging his head from side to side. I hardly recognized him. I had the feeling he hardly recognized himself.

"No? I can wear the suit without the tie?"

How the hell did I know?

"Uhm… sure."

"Yes. It's probably better." He sighed and looked over at me. "Well… shall we make our grand entrance?"

He let me go out first and followed me with his keys in hand. His eyes darted out to the street and then back to the door, he locked it, and then shook the door by the handle to make sure.

"So, where to?"

"Just a couple of blocks." I tried to look cheerful to balance the stiffness of his face. "It's a nice day, isn't it?" New York in July is always hot. Mercifully, it was not humid. He squinted as he was ejected into the outside light. The air was still but this tiny side street was filled with trees in full leaf and the world took on a green complexion. It seemed to slow the movement of the occasional car that strayed past. I wondered if he got nervous when he used to perform but this didn't seem like the right time to ask.

"I was thinking about what you said last time about talent."

He seemed distracted. Looking all around. It almost seemed like he was trying to decide if he enjoyed being outside.

"Oh really? What did I say?"

"Well… about how there are a lot of talented people out there who we never heard of." He was still looking all around him. I wasn't sure he had heard me. "So, I was watching this Rice Krispies commercial—"

"A what?" He reawoke.

"Uhm… A television commercial? For breakfast cereal?"

He nodded rapidly. "Ohhh!"

"I mean, I've seen it a hundred times and the song—the jingle—well, it's got this pretty smart music in it. But it finally hit me. The guy who wrote this thing is a… well, he's got to be a talented musician. I mean the whole thing sounds like a three-part invention."

He smiled. "And if you've seen it a hundred times, he's probably doing all right."

"Huh?"

"Financially."

I felt myself squint. "You mean it?"

"Sure, probably. But I'll bet you he's not playing commercial jingles in the evening with his friends."

I thought of my mother. "He's playing chamber quartets… or something." That made me sad. Who grows up dreaming of writing tunes for breakfast cereal?

Mr. Kreitz saw my face. "Hey, he could be selling ice cream on a street corner somewhere. Then where would he be?" He looked at me again. "You don't seem to take much comfort in that. Please understand, Michael. I don't want to discourage you from becoming a full-time musician. I just want you to know what you're getting yourself into. It's not the easiest life."

I thought about that. "C'mon, Mister Kreitz! Wasn't

it great being famous? I've heard people talk about it. There's a table for you at every restaurant in New York. You can get tickets to everything. Everyone wants to know you—"

"Everyone wants to know you. And that's a good thing? I once told you I didn't like going outside. You probably thought I was one of those people who's afraid of his own shadow. That's not it. I couldn't walk out the door without being attacked by people who thought they were my friend, or wanted to be. I got tired of the autographs, tired of the empty chat, tired of the meaningless, useless requests. I didn't have a moment to myself, a moment *to be* myself. It was exhausting. I started hating people. I finally started hating being me. Do you want to be famous? Really famous? So then, how do you know if someone likes you for who you are or just because they heard you make nice music somewhere? Or worse. The people who haven't even heard you play music but just get horny from knowing famous people."

Horny?

"And now we're going to see my mother."

Long silence.

"Michael—"

"It's OK."

"Michael, I'm going to see your mother because I like you. Because I think of you as a friend and you asked a favor of me. Because I think you're a good person so I can only imagine that she's a good person, too."

I wanted to say *Don't get your hopes up.*

It was eight steps up to the front door of our

brownstone. I bounded up the stairs two at a time as I always did and then looked back to see him sidle to the bannister to make his slow climb. The railing consisted of painted pipes connected to vertical pipes sunk into concrete-filled holes in the steps. I pretended to be distracted by a bird. He got to the top and gave what I can only call a triumphant sigh.

There was an outer door with glass panes that needed unlocking, then a vestibule just large enough for mailboxes, doorbells, and an intercom. Then another door but operable with the same key. I held the doors long enough for him to pass through and then let them fall shut. I didn't watch him but felt glad that we didn't have to climb any more stairs to another apartment.

It was usually quiet in this hallway. The floor was tiled and the walls were covered with plaster so it was hard to hear anything from the apartments upstairs. But there was sound coming from behind our door here on the ground floor and that wasn't right. The agreement was that it was to be my mother and Mr. Kreitz. Even Simon would be gone, or in his room reading. Mr. Kreitz did not seem to notice, or otherwise he was being polite. I felt my heart pound as I sawed the key into the lock.

I could hear a few voices—a man laughing. I looked back. Mr. Kreitz gave a nervous smile and said, "My, my! Your mother certainly has a deep voice!"

I could not return the smile. There was more laughter and now I recognized the voices. They were the members of my mother's quartet. Yes, they were musicians. Yes, they were nice people. And, no, this was not the agreement.

I took us through our door and led the way into the living room. The table had a tablecloth on it. The only time I had seen that was at Passover. It was covered with dishes of canapés and hors d'oeuvres, a dozen or more wine glasses lined up neatly, and bottles of red and white wine.

Not a minute after we came in, the doorbell rang. My mother rushed past me to our intercom to buzz someone in without finding out who it was and slid the doormat under the door. The quartet members all gave me a cheery hello and all I could think was, *You should at least feel embarrassed for doing something you know is wrong.* Clearly they did not know and I realized, of course, that my mother had not told them she was breaking the rules. After greeting me, they fell silent. Then, slowly and hesitantly, the violinist, Gerald, extended a hand to Mr. Kreitz and introduced himself. The violist and cellist did the same. Their movements were so strange. They were adults trying to pretend that they weren't children.

Mr. Kreitz took each of their hands and said, "How do you do," and, "A pleasure." There was the thinnest smile on his face, but I knew this expression. It was the look he gave me when he thought I was lying. Like the time I told him his piano sounded beautiful when it was really so painfully out of tune.

A couple came in behind us. There were sounds of kisses and the exchanging of gifts and, *"Oh, you shouldn't have!"* I knew these people, too. They were also musicians. Of course, my mother knew lots of musicians, but were they *all* going to come?

So, now there were five guests but I had already counted at least twelve wine glasses. Should I grab Mr. Kreitz and push him out the door? Should I apologize to him? Or was he all right? Maybe he was enjoying people after having been away so long. Before I could do anything, the cellist had corralled him and brought him over to a big easy chair that we had at the far end of the living room. Someone offered him a glass of wine. Someone else offered something to eat. Everyone bearing gifts to Kreitz. The doorbell rang again. I had not moved from my spot and people had to push past me to come in. Something else I noticed—all the men were wearing ties. They never wore ties. I thought of his tie now lying on his couch. More people came in. Guests were pulling up chairs in a semicircle around him.

My mother walked past me into the living room and without thinking I grabbed her arm with two hands. She turned around and gave me this haughty look straight out of an old movie—the ones where everyone is wearing top hats and lots of jewelry. She wrenched her arm away and, without making eye contact, said, *"Michael, please!"*

She was wearing what she called a pencil dress. It forced her to take stupid little baby steps when she walked. Her hair was set in a pageboy which made her look ridiculous.

I followed behind her and whispered, probably a little too loudly, *"What's going on?"*

She looked ever so slightly offended, checked around her, and whispered, "It's fine, Michael."

I knew it was anything but.

The living room continued to fill up. When we had

parties, people would inevitably filter off into the kitchen to have more space, but no one was doing that, here. Some couldn't even make it over to greet Mr. Kreitz. I moved away from the door because people kept bumping into me, but I stayed far away, against the wall, unable to do anything. I was watching this scene and still I could not believe it.

"Who is your favorite composer?"

"Well, I don't really have one."

"So, what was your favorite piece to play?"

"Again, I never really had one."

A woman stood up and pushed a tiny photograph at him. "I took this of you at your dressing room door in Carnegie Hall when I was eighteen." He skewed his head sideways and squinted but clearly didn't recognize anything in it. He tried to smile and nod.

"Where was the craziest place you ever played?"

"Crazy? I can't really think of one place—"

"Did you really have a big argument with Stokowski?"

"Oh, I don't know if…"

There were now four glasses of wine on a little table next to him, none of which he had touched. He looked at his wristwatch. I looked at the clock on the wall. About twenty minutes had passed. People started pulling their chairs closer to make more room—or to make less room.

"So, why did you stop performing?"

"Well, it just got—"

"Is it true you left Moscow right in the middle of the Revolution?"

"That's not completely accurate. I…"

Someone brought yet another dish of canapés over to

the tiny table pushing another dish to the floor with a crash. No one even noticed. His eyes had wandered away from the crowd around him until he found me. His gaze fixed on me. Penetrated me. His face was completely calm but I could see accusation. The tiniest movement of his jaw said, *This is your doing. You are putting me through this.*

Someone touched his sleeve and he startled. "Do you still have your violin?"

"Well, of course, but—"

"I think we have one here. Wouldn't you play something for us? Just one short piece?" The man stood up and shouted behind him, "Gerald, don't you have your fiddle here?"

And, as if by the slash of a conductor's baton, the living room fell silent. There was much shuffling of feet as people started to back away, clear a path down the middle. All I could hear was, "Thank you. Sorry. Excuse me. Thanks. Thanks so much." It was Mr. Kreitz, perspiring and angry. Some people looked away or at their feet. One woman was actually covering her open mouth.

I had never seen his face like this. Lips pressed together. Eyes hard. "Thank you, Michael. Goodbye." His voice was the angry grandfather in *Peter and the Wolf.*

I was frozen to my spot. By the time it occurred to me to move, he was out the door. I followed him but he was already halfway down the outside steps.

"Mister Kreitz… I didn't—"

"Goodbye, Michael." He didn't look at me. I watched

him head down the sidewalk.

I came back into the outer hall to find my mother standing there.

"We had an agreement, Mom! A *very simple* agreement! You and me and Mister Kreitz!"

She stuck her chin at me. "What did you expect me to do? What did you expect me to say to my friends? What did you *expect*? *'I know a secret and I'm not telling you'*? Or, *'I'm having a party and you're not invited'*? What am I? Six years old? So? I told my friends in the quartet! I was thrilled. I had the chance to meet my hero. How would it have been if I had said to them, *'Oh, well, Zhenya Kreitz was here but I didn't tell you'*? How realistic is any of that, Michael?"

All I could do was stare at her.

"Well?"

"You're not even going to say you're sorry."

"*Sorry?* Sorry that he acted the way he did? Sorry that I didn't know he would act that way? Someone who spent the majority of his adult life in public? Sorry that I told some people?"

"Well, I'm sorry I told you." For a moment, she considered the idea but her eyes were still hard. "He told me he hated being famous and now I know why. People he didn't even know were always deciding that he was their friend. Well, he's *not* your friend… and now he isn't mine, either."

"Oh, come on! Just go over to his house and—"

"No, Mom, I can't. You see, I lied to him."

She squeezed her eyes shut and shook her head. "You know, this is just so much bullshit. You should have seen him twenty years ago. Surrounded by admiring fans. All these girls fawning all over him. You should have seen him hating *that!* Have you ever asked him how many of his sweet admiring fans he fucked?"

I needed a door and the one that led outside was closest, so I took it.

⸘

I HAD MY DELIVERY bike chained up to the old wrought-iron fence in front of our building. The fence was built up of a row of spears pointing skyward. As I pulled the chain around, it scraped off a chip of paint and I could see that the black bars had once been painted green and maybe silver before that. It had been painted so many times that the points at the top of the spears were completely blunt and rounded and I wondered if they had ever been sharp—a way of keeping out unwanted guests. I wanted to get a great big file and sharpen the points, the way Gomez Addams did on TV. I threw the bike chain into the delivery basket and rode off.

I made my way to Eighth Avenue and headed north. Fourteenth Street, then Central Park, then Connecticut, then Massachusetts, Vermont, Canada…

The streets were not as busy as they would have been on a work day, but it was never easy navigating the avenues, certainly not on a big, clunky bike. My deliveries never took me more than ten blocks, and then never out of the Village. Now I had made it about twenty blocks and everything felt hard. It wasn't dark yet but I could see darkness coming. Or feel it. Out here in the world I realized just how small I was, how little control

I wielded—over the universe, over my life. My smallness was the dominant force in my existence. The world was powerful and noisy and jostling and I was small.

And, in all this noise—cars honking, engines revving, people shouting—I realized something was missing. The music in my head, the soundtrack to my life, was gone.

Others might find the constant internal thrum disturbing, never to have their thoughts clear of sound. For me, it was nothing more than how it had always been. Life was unimaginable without my mind-music. Now there was silence inside and I was empty without it. All the noise around me pressed in on my ears with nothing there to push back. The silence in my head hurt my heart. The lack of pressure from within made me feel as if I might implode.

I came to the street where Richie Koestler lived. Maybe I could hang out here for a while. Maybe I could move in.

I found his apartment building and locked the bike to a No Parking sign. I buzzed, announced myself to his mother on the intercom, and made my way inside.

Richie met me at his door looking slightly quizzical. I didn't live so close to him that I ever just dropped in. It was too late for a punchball game. I came in and thanked his mother.

She scanned my face and smiled. "So, how have you been?" Her voice was friendly. I knew she liked me.

"Uh, yeah, fine, thanks." I found it hard to make eye contact.

She paused for a moment. "Well… would you like to

have dinner with us? We haven't eaten, yet."

I felt relieved and embarrassed all at once. "I don't want to just barge in."

She smiled. "Everyone's always saying I make too much food. You can help us eat it all." She turned around and called behind her, "Richard, would you give me a hand in the kitchen for a sec?" He looked at me and shrugged. He followed her through the door and I heard her whisper, "I think he's been crying." I rubbed my eyes and cheeks as hard as I could with my sleeves. More whispering. Then she poked her head out of the kitchen and said, "How about I call your mom to say you're eating here? Would you like to sleep over?"

Adults could be cruel. They could also be all-seeing, kind, and merciful. I just never knew what to expect.

WEEKS PASSED AND the music in my head was struggling to make its return. I was constantly aware of something that was now absent, something I had always relied on—a missing tooth that would not grow back. I tried to supplement it with music from the outside, with records and radio and practice. Even more practice. But to lose my inner soundtrack was to lose a portion of my soul.

Of course, lots of people hear music in their heads. After all, what is happening to anyone whistling an idle tune or humming random notes as they walk down the street or do chores around the house? What is that? Is it a reflection of something inside or are they just random notes? What is the nature of music that we feel the need to sing along with songs on the radio or tap our toes in time?

For me, the difference has to do with where the music is coming from. It is a soundtrack of my emotional state, and I get to listen to it. I wake up hearing music, whether Robert Schumann or Bob Dylan, or an unknown composition—possibly my own. It follows me through my day. It is never so loud as to block out conversation or, perhaps more important, music from the outside. But, the moment the outside world falls silent or loses interest, my inner music seeps back through and makes itself known. Softly always. A tinkling piano in the next apartment. But always there. It would be oversimple to say it is a direct reflection of my mood, which is to say sometimes that's just what it is.

There is another difference: mine never stops. Except that that's not true. It did stop and I thought it might never come back.

{

MY MOTHER AND I stopped talking. She worked and cooked. I practiced and ate.

I continued making deliveries at the delicatessen, though I asked Mr. Kahanah to take over the Friday pot roast delivery to the Hermit. I always found a different excuse and he always gave me a bright smile and said, "Sure thing, Chief!"

On other days I played punchball. I stopped going for the easy hit. Instead, I tried to catch the Spaldeen on my middle knuckle—really whack the thing—so the ball would sail out to the fence. I didn't care if the outfielder caught it. I just wanted to hit as hard as I could. To my surprise, it offered solace. I could get caught up in the excitement of the game—punch and run and throw and argue and spit and swear and fill the silence.

But I was talking less to my school friends and making more space for the piano. Over time, my participation in playground games became a formality. A gesture. A nod to the fact that we had once been friends. Some days consisted of nothing more than "Hi, Mike" and "Good hit" and "See ya 'round."

Invitations to weekend parties also slowed. My ability to play guitar was not enough reason to keep me close.

I took my earnings from the deli, so carefully saved for more music, and bought five Spaldeens. I went to the Gansevoort Street playground when I knew there would be no one playing, before lunch or after dinnertime, and just tried to punch them from one fence to the other. The pink rubber balls started out with a pleasantly smooth surface, almost like peach fuzz, and smelled of new pencil eraser. After a few hundred punches, they darkened in color, became hard and shiny, and more difficult to hit. My arm began to ache from all the punching. But, when I finally lost one over the fence, car drivers either yelled, *Hey, be careful, will ya?* or *Nice hit, kid!* One guy shouted both.

But when the punchball stopped and it was time to go home, the angry grandfather from *Peter and the Wolf* returned. I thought of avoiding the piano but could not. We had grown too close. Until the music inside finally did decide to come back, I would have to fill it from the outside and the piano was always there to help. Anything, anyway, to keep the old man out of my head.

At some capricious moment, of course, the internal soundtrack finally did return. It was bound to happen. By the time I noticed its presence, the sounds had already been in place for some time. Its own Surprise of… *Of Course!* It was just a question of my waking up to them. Thinking, *Hey, you're back! I didn't hear you come in.* It took a seat in the rear of my consciousness, careful not to disturb the ongoing performance, excusing itself to neighboring thoughts, apologizing for stepping on any toes.

In perfect counterpoint, the old man made a silent exit from my daily thoughts.

$\wr$

WHEN MUSIC TAKES an unexpected turn—for instance, when you change keys—you cannot just return to the start anytime you want. It does not work that way. You have to go through a variety of steps that finally take you back to the original key, if that is what you want. Tonal attraction can take you up or down. But, to get back to where you started, you have to play through a set of other changes, pass through other doors—false cadences, secondary dominants, a circle of fifths—to take you back. Along the way, those sounds will fool you into thinking, *Ah, this is where I wanted to go all the time*. Another Surprise of… *Of course!* And, even then, because the music has gone through all these permutations, the place you end up at will never really be the place where you started, because you have experienced so much in the interim.

My life had taken an unexpected path. Followed a deceptive cadence. Not the line I thought I was following. This was a new feeling for me.

I had never missed my father. I did not miss my mother when she was away for a few days or more. I did not miss my cousins, though they lived far away. I was always happy to see them, but I did not long for their presence when they were not around. I thought—or thought I thought—of myself as complete in myself.

It wasn't like I was prepared to launch into a chorus of "I've Grown Accustomed to His Face." But I was now aware that Mr. Kreitz had changed my daily routine. He had changed my entire balance. The way I thought about music. The way I thought about most things. And now, in his absence, he had changed it again.

Why had I made him so important? What had I done to lose him? Sure, my mother had been an asshole, but I could have seen it coming. I *should* have seen it coming. And *he* could really be a pain in the ass, too. All his questions. Why do we love music? How does music make us feel emotions? *What is music?* If I'm honest, I still don't know.

⸮

MY MOTHER'S ABSENTEE notes started showing up more often, sometimes a few times a week.

MAC-CHEESE IN THE OVEN

and

TV DINNER IN THE FRIDGE

and

JACK IS TAKING YOU TO THE WAVERLY DELI FOR DINNER

I didn't mind her absences. It was cheaper than running away from home. And, let's be honest, I wasn't brave enough or stupid enough to do that. I had seen teenage kids living out on the street. Panhandling for change, sleeping in doorways—filthy, dispirited, betrayed. If nothing else, I could not exist without my piano. As long as my mother paid for my creature comforts, I'd take them.

But I also knew that other kids had parents and families who gathered around the TV after dinner. Played Monopoly. Had milk and cookies. Built model airplanes with Dad. Played catch with Junior. You could see them in magazine ads and TV sitcoms. The idea of my family even approaching anything like that was something beyond laughable. Simon was making himself even less available. He was at City College more or less full time, and working when he wasn't studying, and hanging with friends when he wasn't doing the rest. He had found his comfort outside the house. The more power to him.

When we did eat dinner together, we kept conversation to the essentials—business affairs. Scheduling. So my mother was clearly surprised when I asked her a personal question.

"So, Mom, all these evenings when you're out. I'm curious to know what you're doing. I mean, where do you go?"

The tiniest lift of her chin said so much. It built a wall. The kind that says, *I don't have to answer to you.* I had to struggle not to look away. Pretend I hadn't seen it. She considered the question. Or rather she considered not answering.

"Gerald, our violinist—"

"From your quartet."

"He organizes gigs for us."

"Gigs?"

I knew that the word was not reserved for rock musicians, but she was using it to be self-effacing.

She smiled, the tension was defused, and I could breathe out. "Turns out he has connections among the New York Rich. Somebody gives a party in Lenox Hill? They want a quartet. A gallery opens an exhibition in the Heights? Same thing." Clearly, she enjoyed telling me this and I could just nod along. "All we have to do is play and all they have to do is pay. Easy." She sat back.

"Anyway, I think you know I've been wanting to perform more. We all have." The *we* in that sentence clearly did not include me.

I put on a bright smile. "Cool!"

Then silence.

"Uhm, do you think I could come hear you sometime?"

"No." Her answer came a little too fast. Was she expecting the question? "Sorry, these are private affairs. I don't think they want people hanging around."

By prohibiting my access to her, she was excusing herself from being part of my audience. I realized I had never expected her to see me play. In fact, I could hardly imagine it. And, by not expecting her to show up, no expectations had been betrayed.

No surprise there.

Somewhere in there I imagined she was considering thinking about formulating some kind of apology for not being more present as a mother, or anything else, but I'll never know for sure.

ʅ

I DID NOT MEASURE my life so much in birthdays as in musical pieces—from Beethoven's *Pathétique* on to the more difficult sonatas, to the Schubert Impromptus. Then up the steep hill of the Chopin Etudes—not all of them; some were just too difficult—and up to the moderns: Scriabin, Bartók, Ligeti, and far worse. I was making up for lost time—playing catch-up. The children on Leonard Bernstein's Young People's Concerts had started their frantic practice at age eight, or age three. I awoke at thirteen and was only getting up to speed by age sixteen. It was too late to be a prodigy.

Richie Koestler and Donny Eisenstadt continued to be loyal friends, and they understood that I had something important to do other than play punchball. So they showed up dutifully on my birthdays and I took them to the movies. They would then sink away into their real lives, and I into mine.

Another year passed. I was still getting lousy grades at school. There did not seem to be enough hours to do homework and practice piano. I had to stop working at the deli. I missed hanging out with the Kahanahs and getting free sandwiches, and I really missed that enormous delivery bike. I didn't really care about the bad marks and, to my surprise, neither did my mother—which is to say she had almost no comment about much of anything in my life.

There was one event, or nonevent, that had insinuated itself into my life. Actually, *anti-event* might be better because it was not something happening, but something *not* happening. And again, not so much an event as a trend. In retrospect, I think it should have been obvious, because it is now.

The Surprise of… *Of Course!*

My mother was receding into the background. It was the most gradual movement on her part. So graceful as to be invisible. The most fog-like disappearance. I think I just assumed she was there… until she wasn't. Had she ever been there? That was what I could not figure out.

Sometimes there was a faraway voice saying "I'm going out" followed by the *click* of the front door. Sometimes I headed to the kitchen to find the house otherwise devoid of life. I did not take it personally. I did not know how these things went in other homes. Probably just like here, I assumed. Probably. It's hard to notice something that isn't there.

I knew I was entirely absorbed in my practice and, even if I had noticed any change, I would have marked it down to a normal state of evolution between parent and child. Children require more space as they grow. Parents back off. There is no buried meaning.

But the anti-event followed a specific course. My mother nagged me, pleaded with me, threatened me for years to practice the piano. When I did start practicing—

and when I got good at it—she started her exit. There were fleeting moments, when I came up for air, that I could see (or could have seen) a perfect parallel between my approaching musical success and her increasing disappearance. I just didn't put it together.

"I'll be home late. See you after school tomorrow." *Click.*

I know this about myself. I would prefer to get all congratulatory in my memory of myself—to imagine how terribly clever, how insufferably precocious I was as a child. I wasn't. I was just some kid. I hated school. I perceived adults as beings from an alien planet. I didn't change my clothes often enough. I cheated on brushing my teeth. I thought "Hogan's Heroes" was just hilarious.

Here is what I know now. Musical families are an unusual bunch. It's a hard life so everyone needs as much support as possible. They stick together. Encourage each other. Share ideas. Comfort each other at difficult moments. Take joy in one another's successes.

Click.

}

MY MOTHER'S SUNDAY morning brunches continued, no matter what. There were more political problems than ever to solve. Johnson had given way to Nixon and Vietnam raged on.

In 1964, Mississippi State Police had found the bodies of three civil rights activists dumped in a swamp. Three years later, after the State of Mississippi refused to prosecute the case, the United States federal government charged eighteen individuals with "conspiring to violate the constitutional rights" of three civil rights activists, a charge that carried relatively light sentences. Seven were convicted. The other suspects were let off.

This was the Summer of Love.

WINTER BECAME SUMMER became winter became summer. Simon and I joined our cousins up at the Lake. My mother stayed behind and that was fine with us.

It was to be my last visit to the Lake. I knew it on some level because I was going into my last year of high school, but the idea never fully registered. I don't think I could imagine places to which you never return—certainly one as familiar and friendly as this. Still, I felt myself trying to memorize the smells of spruce and cedar, the isolated calls of birds and frogs, the hiss of trees around the lake, the *ostinato* of water lapping up on the beach, against the boat hulls. Across the lake, I could see lights going on in houses as evening arrived. I had become used to my own company and enjoyed sitting alone on the boat rental dock, watching stars make their appearance.

I did feel nervous about not having a piano to practice. The piano in the cottage was unplayable and anyway the cottage walls and windows were too thin. I also suspected that, the moment I started practicing a Chopin Etude, the other kids would stop using it to play "Heart and Soul" and "Chopsticks" and "Down at Papa Joe's." So I comforted myself with the idea that air and water and human contact would be healthy substitutes. It was only four weeks.

In anticipation of our trip, I put new strings on my guitar and took it along. I had to play music, but I also had music to play. There was always Beatles and Stones, Dylan, Marvin Gaye, Martha Reeves, Smokey Robinson, the Kinks, the Byrds. I hadn't played the guitar in a while but I noticed that all my piano practice had made the guitar playing easier in another way. I no longer had to think *this goes from C Major to A Minor* or even *I have to drop by a minor third here*. The sound went from my ears straight to my fingers.

I did not know the lyrics to a single song. I was not listening closely enough. But I knew all the music—I had no idea how, except that it was all around me. Simon had his mini-stereo tuned to one of the pop stations. One of the kids always had a transistor radio going after school. So the music went in. Sitting around the campfire, someone only had to sing the first line of "Brown Eyed Girl" and, sure enough, someone else knew the second line. And everyone knew the chorus. All I had to do was fill in the music. And faces would light up. That was what made the party. That was the magic.

On Simon and my last night at the Lake, all the teenagers gathered for a party down at the fire pit. Several kids checked in beforehand to make sure I didn't forget the guitar. Some brought hotdogs, others brought beer or sweet wine, there was a giant pan of peanut butter cake, someone brought a handful of joints. There were the ever-present marshmallows for roasting on green twigs. We sang, we ate, we got stoned. The fire exploded and popped in agreement. Never have I talked about absolutely nothing for so long and enjoyed it so much. The late-night air turned cool and damp and, still, we never wanted it to end.

When all the food and dope was gone, when all the songs had been sung, kids started to get up, stretch, and yawn. They thanked me for the music and the others for their contributions. The city kids headed back to their cottages and townies went back to their homes.

I was always slow getting up to go. To this day, I'm one of the last to leave a party. One girl, Amber (or was it Jade?), stayed behind. She sat on a felled tree trunk close to the fire, now reduced to embers. She hugged her knees and watched me.

"Play 'In My Life' again."

I looked around. It was just the two of us. I had stopped playing and realized just how chilly it was.

"Really?"

"Please? Last time."

It really was the last time. Anyway, I loved an audience. Oh, why not?

I sang it, again, though differently this time. This time I sang it for one person. I tried not to make eye contact,

We were silent for a moment, letting the music soak into the trees until the crickets resumed their song.

She held out her hand. "Come on, I'll walk you to your cottage."

The next fifteen minutes was a succession of fumbled buttons and caught zippers, belt buckles digging into legs, bumped noses and missed kisses, sweat and drool mixed with earth and leaves, an accidental elbow to the ribs, some embarrassed laughter, grunts and gasps, heaving and panting—all resembling something not entirely unlike sex.

The next morning, Simon and I were back on the train to the City. Simon was absorbed in *Cannery Row*. I sat quietly, watched the world rush past, and all I could think was, *What did I do to deserve that?*

SCHOOL PASSED UNNOTICED. I settled into a new rhythm—school followed by piano practice and regular performances with local orchestras. I saw my friends less often. I thought of them as friends, though that idea may have just been born of the wish not to think of myself as without friends. I did not want to think of myself as a recluse. But the autumn and chill wind called for touch football, which I did not like, not least because I worried about hurting my hands. So I sat with those kids whom I thought of as friends at lunch break in the school cafeteria, and they seemed glad enough to have me there, though that was starting to become my only form of contact with them.

IT WAS STILL MY task to pick up the brunch food at the delicatessen while my mother tidied the house. One Sunday, I entered the store to a big *Hello!* from Mister Kahanah, bigger than usual.

"Hey, I got a special delivery for you, here." He smiled.

"What? Who from?"

He shrugged. Obviously he knew. "Take a look."

It was a manila envelope, glued shut. I tore it open as carefully as I could manage and pulled out a booklet of four pages. As soon as I saw the yellow-and-green cover, I knew it was sheet music. The front read:

J.S. Bach

**Orchestersuite Nr. 3, D-Dur, BWV 1068, II. Air
Bearbeitung für Violine und Klavier**

Paper-clipped to the front was a note:

> *MAYBE MUSIC IS A LANGUAGE AFTER ALL.*
> *SHALL WE TRY?*
> *E. KREITZ*

⸮

WE LOOK AT A favorite tree, maybe one close to where we live. We admire it. We rely on it being there. We might even make friends with it. And, maybe, forget about it. After all, it's only a tree. Then, as summer moves to autumn, we look back and see it has changed. The leaves are changing color. It might even smell different. When did that happen? We look again and the winter has changed it again. The leaves are gone. There might be frost along one side. It could have died for all we know, or maybe it is just in its winter sleep. But, while we were minding our own business, the tree has made its own history. Continued its life. Inched slowly toward death. But, you only notice it when you look away and then look back.

I had not thought about Mister Kreitz in months, or was it longer? I had not seen him in close to three years. How did that happen? When had I stopped thinking about him? He was still there, obviously. But I had forgotten about him. No, that's not right, either. I never forgot him. But I had managed to stash him somewhere out of reach of my daily awareness. Put him somewhere safe, where he could not keep tapping me on the shoulder every time I sat down to practice. He was always there, somewhere. The only thing that had changed was my memory.

⁊

I BROUGHT THE sheet music to my next lesson with Lily, careful to remove Mr. Kreitz's note before returning the score to the envelope. She took it out, looking slightly puzzled—looking back and forth between the music and my face.

Maybe I could divert her attention. I turned my back to hang my jacket and hide my face.

"Lily, have you ever heard of Eugene Kreitz?"

"Are you kidding? I was *in love* with him."

All I could do was squint—trying to see through to the past. I looked at her in surprise. "You…?"

"No, we didn't date or anything, if that's what you're thinking." She giggled. "No, he was a teen idol when I was young. I'm older than your mom, don't forget, and he was a little older than me. I was a young musician when he hit the scene. Dozens, *hundreds* of us would line up for hours to hear him. Town Hall, Carnegie Hall, the Brooklyn Academy—wherever! He was a miracle to listen to… and not too hard on the eyes either."

I could hardly imagine that any of this had to do with the little old man who lived alone and ate the pot roast I brought him every Friday evening.

"Girls would wait at the stage door with their programs and pens hoping for a glance and an autograph. Some would come with bunches of flowers. Some would put on fresh lipstick and unbutton the tops of their blouses. I can tell you, that was not done back in the day."

"You mean he was like The Beatles?"

"Well, in a way, yes. Of course, we also had Frank Sinatra and Bing Crosby for popular music. But, for those of us who had broader musical tastes, Kreitz was something of a miracle. He made music the way we all *ached* to make music." She sighed and smiled. She might have even blushed. "He had quite a following." She thought for a moment. "Did you find him in your mother's record collection?"

"Uhm, yeah." I hated lying to Lily. She deserved better. And I was so bad at it. But Kreitz belonged to me.

She looked at the sheet music again, thought for another moment, and then started to laugh out loud. "You're playing with Kreitz." She had to sit down because she was laughing so hard. She wiped away a tear. "You're in deep shit now, kid." She was now doubled over in laughter. She waved me over and hugged me around the waist, but she couldn't stop laughing. "You should've seen your face when you walked in." More laughter. "I thought you were carrying your death sentence." She did her best to compose herself but needed to laugh a little more.

"How do you know?" How had I tipped my hand so easily?

"Well, first of all, you're asking about Kreitz out of nowhere—except it's not out of nowhere. Add to that the fact that this was one of his signature pieces. Every time he performed, people begged him to play this as an encore." She laughed again.

Rarely had I felt as stupid—as found out. Still, I failed

to see the humor. She could have just said something like *Oh, how nice for you* or *How exciting that you're playing with my old hero*. She checked my face and managed to simmer down to a giggle.

"Sorry." Another giggle. "It's just… now I'm starting to understand all kinds of things. Is it possible you've known him for a while now? Possibly for as long as you've been that much more devoted to your music?"

"Lily…" I wanted to say *Of course that's not true* but I could not. I did not want to diminish her importance, that did not seem fair. But I could not see any other way around it. In fact, it may have been the first time I had made the connection for myself.

"Sorry." She giggled again. "But you owe me some explaining. I mean, how long have you known him?"

"I haven't. I mean, I have. I did."

"Well, that narrows it down."

Did I have to I tell her of my talks with Mr. Kreitz about music? Did I really have to explain that he really had been my reason for discovering music—*my* music— and not she? No, he had *only* helped me discover it. But now he had been gone for a couple of years. Now I was my own motivator. I would have to explain how we had created a friendship, how my mother had ruined things, how I had come to depend on him and then lost him, how we were trying to patch that up.

Except that I was seventeen. I did not know how to say these things.

⁊

PRACTICE WAS NERVE-RACKING. Without the voice of the violin, I expected the accompaniment to lose its direction. A dog without its master. But something else happened instead. Set free, it turned into a peaceful story with a melody and harmony. It was a complete structure— a song of its own. There was a bigger picture. Bach had been able to see—and hear—beyond the melody. Even so, was I supposed to hear the violin in my head or just make the piano separate and equal? I tried not to worry about it.

I had heard my mother speak of the art of accompaniment. A feeble attempt to elevate, to glorify the position of second fiddle, but it sounded like gibberish. She had said, more often, that it was more difficult to accompany than to lead. She called harmony an exercise in spirituality. Of leaving your own body, your own music—your own *thoughts*, even—behind. Of entering the ears and the mind of the other. Right now I felt none of that. Once again, as with the first Bach piece, I didn't have enough to work with. I was just playing notes, not making music. Lily told me to have faith—whatever the hell *that* meant. So I played the notes and played the notes and played them again. And when my thoughts wandered I tried to wrestle them back—the thoughts *and* the music. The strange part is that the piano accompaniment to Bach's most famous Air is not difficult—not difficult to play, that is, which means it is only difficult to feel.

I CAME INTO Mr. Kreitz's living room as if for the first time and I had to overcome the sense of violating his private space. As a delivery boy I'd had full right of entry into every space. Never have I had so much freedom of movement, welcome in so many homes. Now I felt like a visitor.

The violin case lay on his couch, open, with the instrument on display. I had never seen it before other than in photographs. He had brought it out from its hiding place and I imagined it squinting when he had exposed it to the light after so many years of seclusion.

It lay there just like a hundred other violins I had seen in all the years of chamber music I had heard my mother play, or at the concerts she had taken me to. But it was a different color than so many of the violins I had seen. It seemed to emit a light of its own. Suddenly, I found myself unable to move—walk, talk, look away. There was only the violin.

We both said we were glad to see each other. We were not speaking of our last meeting. His anger and hurt, my embarrassment and hurt.

Mr. Kreitz said something but I could not hear.

He leaned over to catch my eye. "Tea?"

The violin continued to exert its own force of attraction. I could not move my feet or my eyes away. I knew that millions of people had come to hear *this* violin, and the man holding it. Despite all the hours of practice I had put into preparing for this moment, this moment had not existed. I could play my part. I could imagine what sounds my music would make. I could think about my fingers pressing down on the keys and how the piano would respond. Now everything was different. It occurred to me that I would not be playing a different piano, I would be playing a different *piece* than the one I had practiced. It would be the same language yet with another accent. Yes, Lily had played the violin part on the piano, but it was not a violin. And, it was certainly not this violin.

The cup of tea was his best effort to put me at ease, but it only delayed the purpose of my visit. We sat and talked in the kitchen—about my schoolwork, about my piano study—but the words were empty and quickly forgotten. Finally, the tea and the talk would have to end.

I sat down at the piano. My fingers were still flexible from the warm-up exercises I had done at home. I had thanked all that was holy that my mother could not hear me warming up. It would have only caused problems.

I played a D Major scale, two octaves up and down, and it relaxed me. The piano did sound different from any instrument I was used to. It was heavy in the bass. Even the high notes had a thudding sound to them. But I could tell he'd had it tuned again.

"Yes, I know. I hear it, too."

I looked up at him.

"It really needs to be voiced. It's lost all its brightness."

I looked back to find him. He had taken his violin

from its case, and had it in his left hand; in his right hand, the bow and what looked like a small diaper which he held between two fingers. I recognized it. The violinists who played quartets with my mother had these fat little cloths. Mr. Kreitz gave me a big smile, tucked the cloth into his shirt over his collar bone, and rested the violin on it. He took his place along the curve of the piano's hip, a place I had never seen him stand before, but he took full possession of it.

I played an A, one up from Middle A, and made it the fifth step of a D Minor triad. It was what my mother did for her violinists.

He smiled. "Should be OK. I gave it a good, long tuning a little while ago." He giggled. "The strings really protested. *Ai-ai-ai, what are you doing to me?*" he said in a squeaky voice. He smiled at me. "So, shall we give it a shot?"

He put the instrument under his chin, straightened his back, and I watched this tiny, stooped man grow by a foot. Concentration fell across his face. A look of intense dignity—almost royalty—shone from him. For a moment nothing else existed. There was only the unity of the man and the instrument. He stroked as lightly as possible across the open strings with the little finger of his left hand.

I was still taking in the transformation. I think I nodded.

"So, what key are we doing this in?"

"There's a choice?"

"Well, yes. It was written in D Major but some people like to play it in C so they can play it all on the violin's

G string." His shrug showed contempt at the idea. "It's a way of showing off. That's where it gets its nickname."

I looked at him, a little stupidly, I think.

"Air On the G String?" He checked my face for recognition.

I had heard that name before, but all I could think of was a joke I'd heard about a fart in a bikini. I decided not to repeat it.

I doubted my own memory and had to check the key signature. "Uhm… yeah. I learned it in D."

"No problem."

"You mean, you can just switch from key to key like that? I mean you're not even using sheet music."

I could only describe his smile as gentle. "Well, some things you never forget."

You jerk! He's played this thing a billion times!

The moment it grew quiet, I could feel my heart trying to hammer its way through my chest. I knew I was not ready—I never would be. I felt him waiting. I looked at the music and at the keys and at my fingers. There was no way out. I breathed in and out into the keys, through my fingers, as I had learned. Lily had taught me to do this thing with my shoulders that said, *we're starting… Now!*

I had barely come through the first measure, when I heard…

"Just a little slower, please. Less speed, more feeling. Is that OK?"

I pulled my hands back from the keys as if I had burnt them, and I was afraid to touch the piano again. This was all I wanted—to be making music with him. There was nothing else. But I also knew I was playing with someone who had been intensely—frighteningly—famous. Why did he want to play with me? Just some kid. Was he doing me a favor? Or would he stoop to anything just to have a little company? Everything about this moment was wrong. Anyway, this was the speed I had been practicing at. It was a good tempo. What was wrong with it?

"Don't worry," he repeated. "You weren't terribly fast. But you can give yourself more time to let the sound come through. And me. *Tisheh yedish, dalsheh budizh.*"

I realized I had been staring, slightly panicked, at the keyboard. Could Lily have been wrong about this? Could the record I'd heard be wrong? I was trying to imagine what *just a little slower* sounded like. I had forgotten to stop nodding—I was still listening to the music in my head. I think he saw it because he waited patiently. I lifted my hands from my lap and just rested them on the keys for a moment. I tried to remember that this was a *good* thing. That I was doing this because I hungered for it.

"I'll count us in."

I looked up to see him smiling. But he didn't count. He brought the bow to the instrument and inhaled strongly where the pick-up would come.

Isn't a musical instrument an amazing thing! It is capable of producing the most impossible sound. All you have to do is attach it to the right person. And no other person could play this instrument and make it sound this way.

Everything changed. He was right. This was the right

tempo. How did he know?

The room darkened and there was only sound. I had never heard a violin breathe like that. It said *I'm happy to be back.* It said *We are creating beauty.* It said *We belong together.* The violin and the piano danced together. Old lovers who met and spoke fondly. Glad to see each other. Any rancor that might have passed between them had long faded. Only happy memories remained.

We finished—much too soon. The piece is less than six minutes long if you take all the repeats. I sat very still, trying to hold onto the notes before they sank into the walls. I realized I had been holding my breath and finally exhaled. I looked up at him.

He smiled. "How was that?" He was perspiring lightly.

"That's what I wanted to ask you."

"Ah," he let his head rock to one side. "Heifetz once said, 'If I don't practice for a day, I know it. If I don't practice for two days, the critics know it. And if I don't practice for three days, the public knows it.'" He looked at me. "I haven't played for ten years."

"Well… I thought it sounded fantastic." Was I only showing my inexperience? After all, how many violinists had I played with?

"Well, that's very gracious of you." He tilted his head back, as if to listen to something I could not hear. "You know what? Let's play it again."

The second time sounded different.

"That was better." I think he said that. I don't think it was me.

"Let's play it *again*." I think I said that.

We played it nine or ten times. And I realized that, if we had played it twenty times, or fifty times, it would sound different, each time.

Was music truly a language? What I learned that day was that a violin and a piano could express their love for one another.

The next week, we played Rachmaninoff's *Vocalise*. Like the Bach, the notes are not difficult to play, but it does call for very close listening. Its character is so different from the Bach. *Vocalise* is intense where the Bach is considered, stirring while the *Air* is thoughtful. The slightest variation in speed or dynamic changes the entire mood—from sweet to deeply melancholy. Go too far and you'll turn it from passion to sugar syrup. It just depends on what mood you're looking for, and then making it happen.

We played it at least ten times. More, I think.

From there we moved to Bach's first Sonata for Violin and Keyboard in B Minor. *That* was hard to play. I brought him one movement each week. Now we were *working* together—playing it fast, playing it slow, playing it straight, giving it a Romantic twist. Discussing the interpretation of the various passages. It was like playing a different piece each time. But, no matter how you play it, the first movement says, *Hello, old friend*, or, *It's been so long*. Or maybe, *I'm sorry to see you go*.

ꝫ

THE FOUR BEATS of Mr. Kreitz's cast-iron door knocker had become our secret code. In it, I still heard the tympani in the first measure of the Beethoven Violin Concerto, even all these years later. And, in it, he knew who was knocking.

"I've come to say goodbye… at least, for now."

"Where are you off to?"

"I'm going to college next week to register. Then I'll just stay out there until classes start. I have to take a bunch of placement exams. My grades weren't really good enough to get me straight in."

His face showed a panoply of emotions, starting with surprise and ending in a sad smile. "Well, I certainly appreciate your thinking of me."

Mister Kreitz, how could I not think of you?

We were both trying to think of something to say.

"Are you happy about going to college?"

I had not thought about that. I was just supposed to go to college. Happy or unhappy didn't enter in.

"I dunno. I've had to stop my performances—not that there were so many, but even so. I've hardly seen my friends because my mom is making me study for the exams. I guess she's right, but I hate it." I shrugged.

"Anyway, it'll be a way for me to get some intensive music study. But it beats me why I have to take French tests."

He smiled. "French can come in handy… if you plan on touring abroad." He went to the kitchen, weighed the teakettle in his hand, and put it up to boil. "It sounds to me like you've made the decision." He checked my face. "To play. To perform." He saw my face and giggled. "Not so long ago, you had dreams of becoming a famous baseball player."

How stupid that sounded now. What a child I had been. That was three or four years ago.

I considered the possibility that this might be my last visit to this place. I looked around trying to cement the sights and smells into my memory. Nothing here had changed, nothing had moved since my first visit. He wore the same trousers and slippers as ever. It was late summer, so he wore a short-sleeved shirt.

He poured tea for us. Summer and winter there was tea. I actually learned to enjoy drinking Swee-Touch-Nee. He called it *tsvetochniy*—floral.

"What was it like, being famous?"

"Oh, it was fun for a while. More than fun, of course. It was great making money doing what I loved best. It was fun impressing people. They came from miles around to hear me do what was for me the most natural thing. It was great to see them thrill at the things I found so easy. Even kitschy things. Do you know what kitsch really means? It means crap scraped from the street. I was playing garbage for people and they were gasping!" He took his face in his hands and rocked his head side-to-side. *"'Oh my goodness, will you listen to that?'* Everyone wanted to be my friend. People gave me things—records, flowers, all kinds of things. They invited me to parties. I heard people say, 'I would never have come to this party but I heard that you would be here.'" He examined my face. "What's up?"

I didn't realize my face had changed. "Sometimes I think it's my guitar that gets invited to parties. Not that I mind so much."

"Yes, I know that one." He banged his teacup down, a little too hard, got up from his couch, and started pacing slowly. "At the beginning I played everywhere. I wasn't going to be one of those stuck-up performers who only played for money. I would play for the people—a noble Socialist ideal—until I realized I was actually paying to play for them. Then, one time, I showed up at a party without my fiddle and, all of a sudden, I wasn't quite as welcome. Eugene, the *violinist* was welcome. Zhenya, the *person* was not."

"You mean they didn't like you?"

He smiled a little sadly. "I don't really know. People asked me everything about what I did and thought but no one was particularly interested in the answer. They weren't interested in who I was. They tried to engage me in the most inane conversations. Finally I realized they were only trying to show me, and everyone else, just how smart *they* were." He turned and looked at me. "So, is it fame you want?"

Of course, I wanted to be famous. But I knew that was not the right answer.

He did not wait.

"I was famous but my fame had nothing to do with me—with who I was. It wasn't me. I only represented something in their minds. Fame was the price I paid for doing what I loved to do."

He was still pacing. I wasn't sure if he was still talking to me, but I let him continue.

"Fame has very little to do with who anyone is. People wanted to warm themselves by my fire. They liked themselves better if they were with me. Or they thought they did. Or whoever they thought I was. Women wanted to be with me. Beautiful women. They more or less threw themselves at me. In my young years, at least." He awoke from his dream. "Am I embarrassing you?"

I was trying not to imagine it. "No, go on."

He didn't hesitate. "Women who didn't know me still wanted to sleep with me. Maybe they thought they knew me, or someone they wanted me to be. But they just wanted whatever they perceived as my power. As if, by sleeping with me, they could take in my power. They wanted my gas in their tank. I don't mind telling you it sounded pretty good to me and I took advantage of it. I put my nozzle in those tanks a few times—more than a few. I didn't hesitate to fill them up. As many as I could for a while. Plenty. Ah, I see I've made you blush. Even so, I bet it sounds pretty nice to you, doesn't it? The *fame*. The *girls*. I can imagine it would sound good."

Happy, slightly confused memories of Jade arose in me. Or was it Amber?

"Well, it was fun… until it stopped being fun. Until it started feeling hollow. At some point I realized it was all meaningless. The women didn't come back for more when they realized I really couldn't fill them up. Not really. Everyone wanted something from me, but no one wanted *me*. I had a million friends, and I had no friends."

"Is that what being famous is always like?"

He thought for a moment. "I don't know. I didn't know how to change it, if that's what you're asking. Sleeping around didn't help. *Not* sleeping around didn't help, if that's what you mean."

"Everyone I know wants to be famous. All my friends want to be Rock 'n' Roll stars or famous baseball players."

"But why? *Why* do they want to be stars? Is it so they can attract attention? Will it allow them to perfect their craft?" He sat again—his thinking place. "You know, I created a name for myself pretty young, so maybe I didn't know anything else. But it makes me wonder. Why does anyone want to be famous? Is it the recognition? Is it respect?" He looked at me. "Is that what you want?"

"Well, I guess I've imagined being a famous pianist."

"Really? How about just being a great pianist?"

"Well, except, wouldn't it kind of stink to be a great musician if no one *knows* you're a great musician?"

He chuckled. "Good point! But, Michael, at some point you'll have to understand that it's not about the fame. In fact, the fame spoils everything."

I had to stop and take this in. "Did you stop because you didn't like being famous?"

He gave me a hard look. "Michael, how can you even ask me that? I was doing what I loved most. There was only music. There *is* only music. Of course, the fame afforded me many things. I could perform where I wanted to. I could *not* perform where I didn't want to."

"So, what happened?"

His whole face changed. Was that anger? Was it sadness?

"I wasn't ready to stop, but enough people seemed to have had enough of me. One day they like you. The next day they don't. I still don't know how that happens."

"Anyway, I wanted to thank you... for the talks. For everything you've taught me."

Except that I did not say it.

२

I WAS NOT ADMITTED to a fancy conservatory because, well, I had not gone to a fancy conservatory before that. At least, that was my logic. As if that weren't enough, the school refused my application for a scholarship, again, because I had not come from a notable place of study. Somehow, my audition tape did not sound as good with that bit of knowledge in the listeners' minds. So I took on a work-study program, which consisted of filling and emptying the dormitory cafeteria's dishwasher a few hours a week. My mother would pay for tuition and books and I would pay for expenses. After my cafeteria shift, I spent my time in classes and in the practice building.

The building was a mishmash of old and new, and in the ugliest possible way—grand oak doors that gave way to fluorescent lighting and linoleum flooring accompanied by the sound of a thousand twangling instruments competing unwittingly with one another.

In the main hall, which led to three stairways—left, right, and center—there was a large bulletin board meant for students in need of rooms or selling old instruments, or the occasional photo of accidental kittens up for adoption. I rarely stopped to look at anything. I couldn't afford anything anyway.

One day, though, two eyes reached out to me from a photo. Someone had hung a newspaper article and pinned a chrysanthemum under one of the thumbtacks. They had written *NY TIMES OBIT* at the top in pencil. It was already a couple of days old…

Eugene Kreitz, Iconic Violinist of 1930's and 40's Career Cut Short by Blacklist, Dead at 74

Violinist Eugene Kreitz, born Yevgeniy Zalmanovich Kreitz in Moscow (U.S.S.R.), has died in his home in Manhattan. The medical examiner constituted signs of a heart attack.

 Kreitz escaped Soviet Russia to the United States shortly after the Russian Revolution and rapidly built a career, performing with all the major American and European symphony orchestras. He was considered one of the foremost interpreters of J.S. Bach of his time.

He was a U.S. citizen for more than half a century.

In 1950, Kreitz's name appeared in the right-wing publication *Red Channels: The Report of Communist Influence in Radio and Television* along with those of musicians Leonard Bernstein and Paul Robeson, actors Charlie Chaplin and Orson Welles, writers Lillian Hellman and Dorothy Parker, and many others. The pamphlet cited Kreitz's "…work for the Soviet Government following the Bolshevik Revolutions in February and October of 1917."

Unlike many of the celebrities listed in the publication, Kreitz was never formally found "in contempt of Congress" before the House Un-American Activities Committee (H.U.A.C.), an accusation that effectively constituted blacklisting. Nevertheless the inclusion of his name next to those who had suffered that charge was enough to tarnish his image irreversibly. Performance opportunities in the U.S. came to an abrupt halt and he was forced to tour abroad almost full time thereafter. He continued performing throughout the early 1950's to dwindling audiences and then went into retirement.

He is remembered by his friends and many fans.

The Friends of Carnegie Hall are organizing a memorial service at…

♩

OF COURSE I'M THE first and only person in the history of humanity to ask this. At least it feels that way, because I'm not satisfied with any of the answers. But, the question is simple even if the answer is not. *What are we after we die?* What do we leave behind? Do we become symbols of ourselves? Are we nothing more than the last, random possessions we managed to hold onto? Furniture in an apartment? Clothes in a closet? Music on a record?

Is even the memory of us who we were? People always say *his memory lingers on* or *she lives on in our memory*. Well, that's unadulterated nonsense. First of all, our memory of others changes over time. Second, my memory of Kreitz is different than your memory of him. And, even if we put everybody's perspectives together, it still wouldn't amount to one complete Eugene Kreitz because they are all—they are only—external memories of the man, or the violinist, or immigrant, or star, or recluse. Because you and I and Kreitz all have things that we have not told anyone. Because we all have secrets.

ʔ

THE RUSSIAN REVOLUTION had calamitous effects throughout Eastern Europe, but its reach did not end there.

Between 1914 and 1917, while military forces in Europe tore each other to shreds—sometimes sacrificing thousands of men to gain a single meter of ground—conflicting emotional and political forces were tearing the United States apart. German-Americans and Eastern-European-Americans did not want to fight against their families or ancestors. Irish-Americans had no desire to help the British cause in the wake of centuries of occupation and rule, culminating in the 1916 Easter Rising in and around Dublin—right in the middle of the Great War.

But American reticence to enter into foreign wars traces back to an old and abiding rule of American isolationism. In his farewell address marking the end of his presidency, George Washington queried, "Why, by interweaving our destiny with that of any part of Europe, entangle our peace and prosperity in the toils of European ambition, rivalship, interest, humor, or caprice?"

The U.S. did not change its stance for more than a century and a quarter. Any suggestion to depart from what seemed to be safe seclusion was thought of as outright treasonous. Watching their European allies lose a generation of men to the meat grinder of mechanized warfare, many Americans fell into a frenzy of xenophobia.

One famous opponent to the war was industrialist Henry Ford who, in 1915, blamed "German-Jewish bankers" for instigating the war, and he had the ear of many of his countrymen.

But antiwar sentiment took a strong turn on May 7, 1915 when a German submarine sank the steamship RMS Lusitania, *killing twelve hundred people. The German military justified its actions based on intelligence that the passenger ship was also carrying tons of ordnance. While the intelligence was correct, the outcome did not plead well in German favor.*

Two years later, the German government commenced "unrestricted submarine warfare." U-boats were permitted, or ordered, to sink any vessel—military or civilian—without warning, and it soon became clear that American ships were high on the kill list.

The tipping point came that same month in the form of an intercepted cable—known as the Zimmermann Telegram—from Germany to the Mexican government promising to help return Texas, New Mexico, and Arizona to Mexican hands—territory it had lost during the Mexican-American War in 1848—if that country would help in the fight against the U.S.

On April 6, 1917, President Woodrow Wilson made a formal request to declare war on the Central Powers, and Congress acceded.

General John "Black Jack" Pershing, commander of the American Expeditionary Forces on the Western Front, chose to ignore the strategic advice of his British and French colleagues and the U.S. Army suffered dire losses early in its campaign.

Another forty-five thousand American soldiers died in the 1918 "Spanish Flu" epidemic (which almost certainly started at an American Army base in Kansas), thirty thousand of whom died before they ever saw combat.

But the only thing people back home saw was tens of thousands of doughboys dying in Europe. Backlash against German- and Irish-Americans was fierce. The overthrow of the Russian Tsar awakened a fear of the rise of Bolshevism in the U.S. Ultranationalism—an amalgam of populism and xenophobia in the guise of patriotism —became the order of the day.

At about the same time, The Protocols of the Elders of Zion, *an unabashedly antisemitic text purporting a Jewish plan for global domination (and, equally blatant, said to be written by Jews) came to the U.S. from Russia. Henry Ford financed its first major distribution in English.*

The teenage Zhenya Kreitz heard these events pass by on the radio, but he had more important things to do. He was making a career. His trip—four years distant—to Paris, or anything following that, was not even a dream.

So the idea of a war a thousand *versts* away was something so abstract as to be unreal. The civil war at home was occupying the attention of every Russian, and he was no different. And there was always his music to keep him busy.

In 1927, writer Dorothy Parker (*née* Rothschild) was arrested at a demonstration protesting the impending execution of Nicola Sacco and Bartolomeo Vanzetti. The FBI branded Charlie Chaplin a "parlor Bolshevik." Orson Welles's name was placed on a list of individuals who should be apprehended in the event of a national emergency. One ultra-right-wing publication wrote of Kreitz, "He fiddled in Soviet Russia while America burned."

In 1943, clergyman Gerald L.K. Smith founded the neofascist America First Party. Shortly after the Second World War he began speaking publicly of the "alien-minded Russian Jews in Hollywood."

Conductor Leonard Bernstein was confronted with his liberal leanings when, in 1953, the U.S. Government refused to renew his passport. Bernstein issued a public apology, claiming his name had been added to a list of known Communists through acts of trickery. He then went on to denounce a number of colleagues as Communists.

In 1923, Eugene Kreitz had been welcomed in the United States as a conquering hero. He served as a great, big, thumbed nose at the Soviet Union—living proof that America was the better place to live, until things started to change. The changes were subtle at the start and less so over time.

Soviet embassies everywhere had requested international news and communications organizations to stop using the descriptor *Russian* and advised them to use *Soviet* in its place. It did nothing to help international relations. It smacked of Bolshevism and that held danger. Kreitz's biographies in concert programs listed him as "hailing from the Soviet Union" or "originally a Soviet citizen" and, by extension, the unspoken connotations began to propagate. And connotations became musings, and musings became whispers.

Kreitz's own Surprise of... *Of course!* was taking shape.

}

SOME OF THE obituary was, of course, nonsense. Filler. I hated it that the *Times* hadn't done its homework. Kreitz did not arrive "shortly after the Russian Revolution." His "many" fans were old or dead. He didn't have friends. He had me.

I hated it that they had given him four inches of ink. How do you reduce a life such as his to a tiny corner of the obit page? How do you reduce any life, but his of all lives? At the same time, I was mildly surprised that a fellow student had known of him at all. Kreitz had disappeared off the map more than twenty years earlier, before some of the people in the music building were born.

I found a pen and a stray piece of paper in my rucksack and wrote, *Who posted this? Please call.* I added my dorm room phone number. I found a stray thumbtack in the corner of the bulletin board and stuck it next to the obit. I wanted to tell someone that I had been his only friend. That he had been my teacher and I had been his final accompanist. That his fame had meant nothing to me. Only his friendship had been important. I wanted to tell someone the truth.

No one called and I felt slightly relieved. I would have had to say that, in all my self-absorption, I had neglected to stay in touch with him in his final year.

I went upstairs for my piano lesson and told my teacher—a graduate student probably five years older than I—that I had known Kreitz. He smiled and said, "Oh, really? That's nice," and then urged me to get on with the lesson.

That evening, I found Lily's phone number in with a pile of papers I had taken to college.

"*Darling!* Hey, I almost called you. Yeah, I saw your mom at his memorial service. Nothing but old farts there. She and I had coffee afterward. I haven't seen that much gray hair in one place since, well, since the last memorial service. It was at that tiny synagogue in the West Village. Seats about fifty shoulder-to-shoulder. But it beats the hell out of me why people feel the need to do these things in houses of worship. He sure didn't give a shit about being Jewish. They found a few amateur fiddle players to come in and play some of the Bach Unaccompanieds. Not great, but nice enough. You saw the *Times* obit? How about that sonofabitch J. Edgar Hoover, huh?"

Why hadn't Kreitz told me? All he had ever said was, "One day they like you. The next day they don't."

𝄐

IN MY SECOND YEAR of college, I found transcriptions of jazz standards by Fats Waller, Art Tatum, Bill Evans, Errol Garner, Oscar Peterson, and a few more, and landed some gigs at restaurants in town. I threw in a Classical piece now and then just to show off my chops. After doing that for a semester, I saved up enough to buy a sixty-three Chevy Impala for two hundred dollars. I started playing nicer places—hotel bars and fancy restaurants—in nearby cities. Those gigs led to studio gigs, and from there to small performance venues. Some were hardly larger than living rooms, just as long as they paid my trip to and from, my meals to and from, and a place to sleep in between.

A year later, I got bored with my study and went on the road. Work was coming in more often, and paying more all the time, and I was missing too much school as it was.

I sent out tapes accompanied by all the positive reviews I could scrape together—and a few I thought up myself—to every small-scale concert hall in the Midwest and further East and followed them up with constant phone calls. Driving endlessly. Staying in cheap motels. Building a name—slowly. It was exhausting most of the time and exhilarating some of the time.

At a given moment, it occurred to me that I was now older than Mr. Kreitz when Sol Hurok had taken him into his stable—one of Hurok's geniuses. So, it was now clear I was no longer the wunderkind—if I had ever been one—and not yet the iconic musician that Kreitz had been labeled. But I could not stop now.

I was not playing the great halls, not yet, but the venues were getting larger—one seat at a time, one town at a time. The travel was lonely, but I was starting to meet some great musicians and that was a thrill.

My big break, if you will, came when the New York Downstate Symphony invited me to play Kabalevsky's Second Piano Concerto. There was something—what's the word?—*ironic,* I suppose about having started my career as a concerto player. I came to realize that most young people did not start their careers playing concertos with orchestras, large or small, although I was not really sure if there was *a way* that all or most young people started their careers. And, again, everything would change when I returned to being a solo pianist. Each step was a step up from its previous place. Being a soloist now was a promotion from having had no recourse but to play alone in the past.

No less ironic, Kabalevsky had been my great enemy at age thirteen, and also the composer who booted me into what would become my world.

I remember the program for that first concert. I'm sure I still have it lying around in a cardboard box somewhere.

> *Michael started concertizing at age fourteen in and around New York City. When asked what he thought brought his early success, he responded, "I was consumed by music. I was obsessed by it from a very young age."*

But, honestly, what a load of crap. What performing musician is *not* consumed and obsessed by music? And who doesn't practice their ass off if they don't think they have half a chance? How much more genuine I would have been if I had said, "Just lucky, I guess." Lucky enough to have the talent. After all, how many struggling musicians out there have everything but the talent? And how painful is that?

‹

ON JANUARY 14, 1975, the House Committee on Internal Security, the final incarnation of the House Committee on Un-American Activities, closed for business. Its work was subsumed into the House Judiciary Committee, but its most reckless and damaging days were over.

A month later, my mother called to say there would be a news retrospective about the HUAC period and she thought I might be interested. I watched just to see if they could tell me anything I didn't already know.

The program turned out to be a closer look at the American Red Scare, the Army-McCarthy Trials—the whole, miserable period. The newsreader billed it as "a hard look at the soul and spirit of our country."

And, sure enough, there was Kreitz alongside so many others—screenwriters, authors, musicians, actors, as well as lawyers and high school teachers—so many of whom saw their careers, and lives, fall apart in the Halls of Congress.

The segment featuring him was short compared to many of the popular heroes, or martyrs, including the highly visible Hollywood figures. The film and sound quality was poor.

The congressman, whose name I don't remember, began his questions.

"Mister Kreetz? Is that correct?"

"Uhh, actually… actually it's Kreitz. Like *cry*."

"Pardon me? Like Christ?"

"No, no. Kreitz. *Kreitz!*"

Even through the grainy footage, I could see the sweat building on his brow.

"What kind of name is that?"

"I don't really know. It was my father's name."

"Is it a Russian name? It doesn't sound like a Russian name."

"I'm sorry, I don't know."

"You were born in the Soviet Union, were you not?"

"No, Congressman, I was not. I was born in Czarist Russia. Tsar Nicholas the Second was, uh, king, when I was born."

"How did you pronounce that?"

"Pronounce what… sir?"

"*Star* Nicholas?"

"I said *Tsar*. It's the more correct pronunciation."

"Ah, well, thanks for enlightening me. So, but you were born in Russia. Is *that* correct?"

"Yes, Congressman, I was."

"And, later, when Russia went Red, you worked for the Soviet Government. Is *that* correct?"

"Well, Congressman, under the Soviet system, everyone worked for the Soviet Government. Either that or you didn't work."

"I see, a kind of company town with a company store."

"I'm sorry, I don't understand."

"Moving on… Mister Crates, are you a Communist?"

"Congressman, it's not… Congressman, no, I am certainly not a Communist!"

"But you were one, we're you not?"

"Well, if you're asking if I was a member of the Communist Party, no, I was not."

"You weren't? I thought everyone was a Party member."

"No, Congressman. I was a member of the Union of Composers and Musicologists, but everyone was—everyone working person in the Soviet Union is—a member of a trade union."

"But you were—"

"Congressman, please let me finish. The moment I left the Soviet Union, I divorced myself entirely from Communism. In fact—"

"But, you—"

"*In fact*, by leaving the Soviet Union without permission, I was placing myself—*and my family*—in grave danger."

"So, you placed your family in danger."

I could see Kreitz's shoulders sag. Damned if he did. Damned if he didn't.

The congressman continued.

"Sir, I understand you are still a musician. Is that correct?"

"Well… to the best of my ability." He feigned a weak smile.

"Yes… and we have already documented a great number of Communist sympathizers in the musical community. You are not a Communist, you say?"

"That's correct. I'm not."

"I see. But, no doubt, you will know some Communist sympathizers, do you not? More than a few. I mean it's hard to imagine that anyone with the number of contacts you have in that world would not know any."

"Congressman, to the best of my knowledge, I'm not aware of any American Communists in the musical community."

"Let me get this straight. Are you saying you know other Communists who aren't American? Or do you mean you know Communist sympathizers who aren't in the musical profession?"

"Sir, I mean to say I don't know any Communist sympathizers, period."

"Your English is really very good. Where did you learn to speak so well?"

"Sir… I…"

"Now, Mister Crates, how can you possibly not know any Communist sympathizers? After all, sir, I'm not even in the musical community and I know—well, or *know of*—quite a few after just two years sitting on this committee."

"Well, Congressman, let me phrase it differently. If I *do* know any Communists, or Communist sympathizers, they certainly haven't told me as much. Most likely they don't think it safe to tell me… if they even exist."

"Mister Crates, do you really think that's likely? I mean, considering your background…"

At this point, the image froze and zoomed in on Kreitz, his face a perfect mix of disgust and defeat. The narrator came on in voice-over.

"That same week, the New York Philharmonic and Chicago Symphony orchestras retracted invitations to Eugene Kreitz to perform. How do you destroy an illustrious career lasting decades in just four minutes? *This* is how. You don't have to convict. You don't even have to indict. You just have to allege. To make oblique association. And, then let doubt and fear run their course. For all intents and purposes, Eugene Kreitz's career had come to an unexpected and sudden end."

⸱

I COULD NOT shake the feeling that, if he had only shared some of this—the rage, the indignation, the hurt—with me, he might have been able to find some peace in his final years.

Until I started wondering if, all that time, he *had* been telling me, or tried to tell me. Had he been screaming in my ear the whole time? *I'm drowning in shame and anger and I only hope you'll hear. Perhaps if I give you the gift of my knowledge and love of music, maybe just being able to watch you succeed in your career will help me to climb out of this abyss.*

ƨ

LOCAL ORCHESTRAS IN the Greater New York area invited me to play with some regularity. I imagined they saw it as a way of consuming local produce—supporting the home town boy made good.

Whenever I was nearby, I'd come into the City, take my mother out to dinner, sleep in my old bedroom, and go up to Lily's for coffee the next afternoon. Lily was getting old—thinner and smaller each time I saw her. She had stopped dying her hair. She had always been thin—one of those people who never had to diet, but now I could see the bones protruding through her hands and wrists. I had the feeling I could almost see right through her, and maybe I could. I thought she might break, or otherwise shrink into nothingness.

It was during one of those visits that a question came to me, clearly one I had been trying to formulate for a while. But, as long as I could see through her, I might know if I was getting the truth.

"Lily, why didn't you send me to a real music school—I dunno, Juilliard, or Mannes, or somewhere? Don't you think it would have made my life easier?"

"*Easier.* Where'd you get that idea? Easier how? And who was I to send you? Ask your mother that."

"I did ask her. She told me to ask you. And you're avoiding eye contact. What is it that no one wants to tell me? I just assumed she couldn't afford it."

"Except that she could afford to send you to college out of state because *they* had a real music school. And, before that, to private lessons every week. And a lot more. Your mom didn't come to me because I was the cheapest around, because I'm not."

She looked across at her apartment and nodded. I followed her glance as if for the first time. It was just her apartment, filled with fine art and heavy furniture. It had only ever been her apartment.

"I can thank your mom, and a few more parents, for this place. But, don't worry. I earned it."

More silence. I think I literally shook my head.

"What are you telling me?"

"You have an uncle, I believe?" *Silence again.* "A rich uncle. Remember him?"

The scales, as it were, fell from my eyes. I think my jaw also fell.

"My Uncle David. I never—. So, what, you got a check from him every week?"

"Oh, not that way. No, he sent your mom money from time to time. Told her to do with it as she saw fit. But I can tell you, it went to you and your brother. Mostly to your music. She told me this after a few too many drinks. She'd kill me if she knew I was telling you now. But maybe that's just what she wants."

"What she wants?"

"Someone who will tell you all this and someone she can blame."

She girded herself for a long story.

"Not so long ago—actually it was after Kreitz's memorial—your mom and I went for coffee. She wasn't done talking so we went out for dinner after that. And then drinks. A regular old home week. Apparently she needed to get a few things off her chest, but it was basically what I've known all along. She couldn't stop herself from competing with you, and she hated that. But, when push came to shove, she gave up everything so you could make your career. I mean, *c'mon,* you don't really think you could have lived in the West Village on her salary, do you?"

"We lived in that crappy little apartment."

"Yup, that crappy little apartment—in the West Village. Not the Bronx projects. But that never occurred to you." She took a sip of her coffee. I could see she was wrestling with a thought. "Michael, your mother saw your musical talent right from the start and she was prepared to give up a lot for it, including her own musical career. I just always assumed you knew, but maybe you didn't. Maybe you don't. Your mom was a good musician. No, not good. She was great—or could have been. But it was a terrible time to be a female musician. The world was only starting to recognize the existence of women as musicians, but with a lot of conditions hooked on. You know, *as long as she's home in time to get dinner on the table.* Well, fuck you very much. If you weren't a singer or a flutist or a harpist—or a music teacher—you were properly screwed. And, by the way, it's still a man who's considered the *only* harpist. Women have to work three times as hard to gain recognition. And, even then, there's something wrong—something odd—about a woman who chooses a career over family." She took a deep breath. "Your mother was faced with a terrible decision, and that took the shape of a sacrifice—a major one." She fixed her eyes on me. "Can you imagine what it's like to trade your life away for the life of another? Can you imagine trading away the career you're having? She took a non-contract teaching job—with a special discount for being female—and was glad to have it. So, yeah, she accepted money from your uncle on the side. And, when that's all said and done, let's not forget what a jackass your dad was. Do you understand what I'm saying?"

"Oh, great. And in return I got a mother who was pissed off at me the whole time I was growing up."

"Michael, I know she wasn't exactly Mother of the Year, but she gave you a home and a family. She could have had a *great* career and she gave it up—for you. Her career had to die so yours could live."

Lily was telling me to rearrange my entire past. I hadn't even thought of my father's contribution to any of this picture. I was having trouble focusing.

"But… well, you still could have recommended me for a proper music school."

"Oh, a *proper* music school. Excuse the hell outta me."

"For godsakes, Lily, every time I played a concert— *for the first ten years of my professional career—* everyone asked me, 'So which prestigious music school did you study at?' And I had to say, 'I didn't. I studied with some lady but you've never heard of her.' I could have had all the extra music theory, composition, arrangement. It would have put me lightyears ahead of—"

"Oh, get over yourself. You did just fine. And, need I remind you, you *are* doing just fine. A *proper* music school would have chucked you out on your ear." She checked my face. "I gave you all the theory and composition you could eat. And I let you back in here— with open arms—each time you didn't practice. Each time you screwed up. You think you would've had that at Juilliard?"

"Is that all there is to it? In that case, what do you need my mother to tell me? What aren't you telling me?"

She glared at me. *"What do you want to hear?* OK, listen to this. I didn't *send* you to Juilliard because I wanted you for myself. All right? Yes, you were all I had amid all those sniveling children who were getting lessons—week after week, month after month—against their will. I was sick of playing piano nursery school. Aren't you glad you're hearing this?"

"Lily, I could have… How could you—"

"What, be so selfish? I had pinned so much hope on you. You were everything I… There we go. I'm getting maudlin, now."

It was as I had thought. She *had* hoodwinked me.

I visited her a few more times because it was the right thing to do, but it was never the same.

ι

I FELT A FRANTIC need to find an adult from my young years who could confirm my past as I knew it. On a whim, I walked around the corner to Jack's apartment. I was not even sure he was alive. He had long since stopped writing for the *Empire Review*.

He peeked around his door and stared at me rather the way Mr. Kreitz had first done all those years ago.

"Michael?" He pulled the door open. "My God, I'd never have recognized you except I've seen your face in the papers. How the hell are ya?"

I smiled. "Come on. I'll buy us a sandwich at the Waverly Deli, if it's still there."

Jack had grown old—everyone had, but I still felt surprised. Rubie had married and moved out from upstairs. Harold, the architect—also of the brunch club—had died a few years earlier.

We walked slowly. I did not mind. I was happy to be with him. The weather was just as I always want it to be in New York—late spring, the trees just coming into bud. My internal music played the opening theme from *An American in Paris*.

We sat and ate our sandwiches. I had coffee. He had a Cel-Ray Tonic—still his favorite. Then he put his sandwich down and looked straight at me. I knew something was coming.

"I better tell you this now, cuz I'm gettin' old and I think you should know."

I had a feeling I did know.

"You and your mom, you had your tangles. But, to me? She was the coolest thing since beer in a can. Smart, sexy, and that lightning wit." He sighed. "I asked her to marry me. More than once, in fact. She said she liked me well enough." He gave a mirthless laugh. "Talk about damning with faint praise. But here's the thing. She said she would have but she didn't want to put you and Simon through it. She said she was bad luck in marriage, that she'd only screw it up, and that would hurt her boys, and she couldn't do that. She said she was crap at showing you, but you meant everything to her." He smiled a little sadly. "Well, I tried to reassure her. Told her I'd make it good. Make it right. I told her what a good team we'd all be. Anyway, that's *that* story. I just thought you should know."

ξ

I HAD NEVER THOUGHT to ask Lily why she had such a grand apartment. I had never asked my mother where and how we lived as we did. I suppose I could have asked her that, too, but did not. Of the people at our Sunday brunch table, I only knew what they did for a living if it concerned me directly. If I cared. Whether they were rich or poor, happy, or unhappy in their lives did not even enter into the realm of my concern. Old people were interesting only in that they were a passing curiosity. Or, I preferred to imagine they were boring rather than presume the only possible alternative: that I was so self-absorbed that anyone outside my age group—and some of those in it—just didn't count. In my old age I find myself wondering if my father's absence from my life taught me to lose interest in old people. They weren't really there, anyway.

A YEAR LATER, my mother phoned to say that Lily had died. I had a week until my next performance, so I grabbed a flight into New York.

I took comfort in seeing so many of her students at her funeral. She had no other family. The memorial service was in a small church around the corner from where she lived. They brought a piano out to the altar and a handful of children and adults played—Mozart's Viennese Sonatinas, the Czerny *Allegrettos*, Couperin's *Barricades Mystérieuses*, even the dreaded Kabalevsky Sonatina—and everyone applauded. It was nice to see. It was the right kind of send-off. Her last student recital.

Then one of the mothers in the audience saw me sitting at the back and, blushing all up and down, asked me if I'd play something. I smiled and I said yes, of course.

I played Chopin's *Nocturne* in E-flat Major. It's popular. In fact, it gets played way too much, but that's how these things go. It's sweet, tender, a little melancholic. The B section contains the loveliest little twist of chords—a tiny Surprise of... *Of course!*

Play it wrong and it's pure corn. Play it right and it's a waltz with an elegant, elderly woman.

Lily gave. Lily took away. Blessed be the name of Lily.

AND SO ADULTS sit with children and pass the music on. The children become adults and pass the music on. And the people change, and the music remains.

Acknowledgments

I am deeply grateful to so many people who taught me about music, about writing, and about writing about music. I hope I have remembered them all here.

Thanks go, first, to my informal (unpaid) music teachers, roughly in chronological order: My mother (*not* Michael's mother) and my father, my sister and my brothers; my cousin, pianist Karen Schwartz, with whom I sang Bach Two-Part Inventions as teenagers, and who *really could* play the Kabalevsky Sonatina; Leonard Bernstein, of blessed memory, for hosting the Young People's Concerts and Harvard Lectures; Melissa Coren; Alan Steinberger; Leo Kottke, who, unbeknownst to him, taught me how to play guitar; John Bucchino; Bart Rademakers; Anne Hodgkinson and Mitchell Sandler, who saved me from some rookie music mistakes; and to Mark Iosefovich Levin for his help with Soviet political and musical history.

Thanks, also, to my formal (paid) music teachers: Rose Cion, Tony Columbia, Messrs. Lindeman and Russ at the High School of Music and Art; Fred Ruf at Far Rockaway High School; and Helga Winold and David Baker at Indiana University.

I also want to thank all the people who give us Wikipedia and YouTube. Without their input, this story would have been nearly impossible to put together.

Special thanks also go to the members of the best damn writing circles in Amsterdam and Maastricht, including (though not limited to) Anne, Ariane, Arianne, Becky, Bob, Colette, Igor, Jelle, Karim, Liz, Martine, Matthew, Mitchell, Norman, Paul, and Stuart. You kept me on my toes and never let me settle for good enough.

I paid particular attention to the lives and work of a few musicians while writing this story: Nathan Milstein, and especially his rendition of Bach's Unaccompanied Sonatas and Partitas; Alexander (Sascha) Schneider, whom I saw play at Carnegie Hall on numerous Christmas Eves together with my (not Michael's) mother; and Berl Senofsky, who won the Queen Elisabeth Competition with his rendition of the Beethoven Violin Concerto, and whom I knew when I was young. I'm happy to say I saw him perform at the Concertgebouw not long before his death.

And, of course, Glenn Gould.

I believe, however, that everyone who makes music has an effect on every other musician. This is how music grows and becomes more beautiful.